CONTENT
MESSAGE

This is a dark forbidden step/adoptive romance with a twist that has content that pushes past forbidden and into tab00.

Please read through all the TW and Tropes before reading this book as there will be content that pushes past social norms. This is a book of fiction and I do not recommend any of it in real life. Your mental health is important, and I do NOT recommend reading without reading the TW list below below.

Step/adoptive romance (but FMC believes they are full-bl00d related. MMC's know the truth)

Twincest (no sword crossing)

Secret birth father

Suicide - off page

FMC sent to an academy as punishment - off page

Child abuse - off page

Beatings as punishment - off page

Food withholding - off page

Arranged marriages

Secret crime society

Cult vibes

Death by childbirth - off page(bleeding to death due to complications)

MMC's see their step-mothers death as being the FMC's fault

Dead mother and step-mother

MMC's mother mysteriously disappeared

Controlling behaviour

Codependency on a twisted scale

MMC's drug FMC

Bad trip on drugs

Blood

Mention of murder-suicide

Graphic Violence - on page

Mental games of manipulation

People held prisoner

Graphic Torture - on page

Graphic Murder - on page

Clothing control

Stabbing

Tongue removal

Cannibalism

Gifting body parts

Knife-play

Blood-play

Chase/Hunting Play while tripping on LSD

Dub/Non-con

Good girl/boy praise

Orgasm denial

Squirting

Biting kink

Bondage

VELKA MANOR
TWISTED BLOODLINE
WINTER BRIER

Copy and line editing by The Fiction Fix

Proofreading by The Fiction Fix

Book Cover Design by Jes Phillips

CONTENTS

Impact-play

Fear-play

Forced orgasms

Fisting

DP

Tattoo against will

Snowballing

Tickling

Ass-play

Marking kink

Carving kink

Owning kink

Big brother/Little sister nickname kink

Ass-play with knife handle

Sharing kink

Cum sharing

DEDICATION

To anyone who likes their romance a push past forbidden and obsessive,

Dorian and Bastian are for you.

I

OCTAVIA

Rain thunders against the car, fog rolling down the hills of the moorland as we speed past. The stars in the night sky that usually shine so brightly hide behind the dark clouds looming above. Lightning cracks in the air, and a shiver rolls down my spine, as if I can feel the icy wind outside cutting my skin. A squeal escapes my lips, and my driver gives the barest of glances in the rearview mirror, shaking his head before focusing on the road again.

My palms sweat the further we go, my stomach swirling with nerves. Every bump in the road makes my stomach drop, and bile creeps up my throat. I can't ask the driver to stop; he wouldn't even if the colour of my skin turned green. Once my father gives someone an order, he expects it to be followed exactly. It doesn't matter if I feel sick or even if I *am* sick. He will deposit me at my home covered in my own sick, another disgrace upon my father's door. I would have angered him before I even arrived. I'd risk being returned to the boarding academy where families send their disgraced bloodline.

I can't go back. I've finally left after three years, dragged out by my arm and thrown into the back of a black Rolls Royce. We've been travelling nonstop for two days, only pausing briefly for restroom breaks and to refuel the car. I might have been upset about the entire thing if it didn't mean I would get to *them* quicker. I wanted to bask in the fire of their gazes and feel the warmth of their skin.

It's been three years since I've seen *them*, three years since my father found the diary where I wrote my deepest, darkest desires, page upon page filled with them and everything I have ever dreamed of them doing and saying. He read it all; he saw my darkest shame, my sickness—every single word.

I never intended for anyone to find it. I don't even know how he did, but I can never forget the disgust in his eyes when he barged into my room and dragged me from my bed, the shame in his tone as he called me a vile disgrace to his bloodline. He slammed my head into the wall, screaming that I was a sick and twisted little girl who needed to be punished. I needed the sickness in my mind carved out.

He beat me black and blue, and in the morning, before even the staff were awake, he dumped me in this very car and sent me away.

"Get her out of my sight. You will never step foot in this house again, Octavia. Not until the brothen's sisters banish the sickness from your mind."

I left the day before my twentieth birthday; I didn't even get to say goodbye to them. They were absent due to work, meeting with the heads of other families. They promised they would be back for my birthday; they never missed it. My father would throw a big party every year with extended members of our family, our bloodline, but then he would leave, and they would do something special for me the next day, just the three of us.

It was always something I loved. It went from teddy bear tea parties to ice skating on the river, and then, on my eighteenth birthday, they snuck me out to a club in a nearby town. That was the year I gave my dark, twisted thoughts a voice. I let the tiny whispers turn into a roar, and I could no longer drown them out. Dancing with them in that club, feeling their bodies moving next to mine, grinding against my back, changed everything.

To them, it was an innocent night dancing with their little sister, trying to show her some fun. But to me, it was the night of my sexual awakening, the first time I acknowledged that I don't look at them like a little sister should. It was the beginning of the end.

I don't know why Father has sent for me now, why he decided that my time with the sisters should end. I haven't cured the sickness; I still want my brothers more than I want air in my lungs. No matter how many beatings the sisters gave me, or how many times they withheld food, my desire never changed. I went along, saying and doing whatever was asked of me, just so I could be with them again. But the sisters were not naïve. I saw in their eyes that they didn't believe me, so why has he brought me back?

Whatever the reason, this time, I cannot slip up. This time, I have to push my sinful feelings down as deep as they will go. The one thing clear to me while I was away was that I cannot live without them. Bastian and Dorian are my black heart and poisonous soul. Without them, life becomes obsolete. Nothing is worth living for if I don't have them. I cannot be separated from them again. If I am, I won't be walking this Earth anymore; there will be no point. Father must believe what I felt has disappeared.

"You're home, Miss Stone," the driver says, breaking me out of my thoughts.

My head whips around, my gaze meeting the dark brick castle now in front of us. The fluttering in my stomach turns wild, my heart beating rapidly in my chest. The driver jumps out, quickly opening an umbrella, shuffling around to open my door. The cold winter air smacks me in the face, goosebumps running across my exposed skin. As soon as my shoes connect with the wet ground, lightning flashes in the sky, thunder rumbling in the air only a few seconds later, and the entrance to the castle slowly cracks open. I shake as I move forward, a foreboding feeling swamping my body. The moorland has welcomed me home with its lightning and thunder; now, it's time for my family.

I feel I am safer with the lightning.

2

DORIAN

B astian opens the door, impatient as ever, and of course, my dramatic twin pulls it slowly, like we're in some horror movie. I'll give him his due—we're not far off. Perhaps less horror and more violence. I doubt they would even show a movie with all the things we do. Our life isn't for the weak; honestly, not even the strong survive here. You have to be a sadistic kind of vicious to thrive in our world. Our reputation is so terrifying, crime lords tremble at the mere mention of our names. Our bloodline breeds apex predators, and the rest get slaughtered. Everyone, that is, apart from our angel.

Our little sister had the misfortune of being born prey, something that would have been wiped out the moment she showed she couldn't stomach the violence that comes with our last name. Fortunately for her, she was born beautiful, something our father took more and more notice of as she grew up. Women in our bloodline receive the gift of being brides, either to the highest bidder or to the last man standing in a room covered in blood. He would have made a lot of money and forged important connections if it wasn't for the simple fact that she wasn't his to give away.

My claim on her happened at birth, the second she came screaming into the world and took her mother from it. Lucinda Stone died before she got to even hold her darling daughter in her arms, bleeding to death from complications. At six years old, I was the first one to hold her and claim her as mine. A saint before she even took her first breath by sending that poisonous woman to her grave.

Technically, my dear sweet sister is more like my step-sister, or adoptive, depending how you look at it. The cunning viper my father married after my mother disappeared was already pregnant. She saw her opportunity to rise higher in the bloodline and grasped it tight in her sharp, red-painted talons. She stomped over the competition, stabbing her Louboutin heels into their backs, all with a sweet smile on her face. My father was obsessed with her, so much so that I've often wondered if *my* mother's disappearance wasn't a calculated plan on his part.

In his foolish want for beauty, he let that viper of a woman make a mockery out of him. She was in the early stages of pregnancy when he declared his intention to marry her. He realised his mistake too late and had to choose between exposing her deceit or acknowledging the child as his own. The former was never an option; he would have lost his standing in the family, demoted to nothing more than muscle and a cautionary tale. He claimed the child as his, and that was it. No one questioned him, so sweet Octavia became mine.

I wasn't the only one who laid claim to her. I saw the twinkle of joy in my twin's eyes as he gazed at our sister, covered in her mother's blood, screaming into the night, waiting for warmth from a woman who would have never given it to her. We were besotted with the little murderer; she was a dark angel born just for us, a sweet doll for two little boys who were desperate for a shining light in a world of darkness.

Father kept her as his daughter; she was part of our bloodline even if she wasn't his. Lucinda was his third cousin, twice removed, and he would never abandon his bloodline, even if he had nothing to do with her. Octavia knows none of this, and that's the way it will always stay.

He left her to the nannies and the help to raise, but he also left her to us. We were the ones he put in charge of her when we were just six years old. We were Stone men in the making and had to learn about the responsibilities our bloodline demanded of us. We didn't get the luxury of a childhood, the comfort of love that a family is supposed to give. We got nothing, but from the moment I set eyes on my dark angel, I vowed she would have everything we didn't. She was mine, and no one was going to take her away.

That thought didn't extend to my brother. He is me and I am him, each one half of a shattered soul. We didn't need to exchange words to know what the other thought; we just knew. That day, whether she wanted it or not, we tied her to us, and no one was going to break it. She was ours to protect, ours to care for, and then, she became more. Our protectiveness changed, our possessiveness developed, she grew up, and she became ours in a way neither of us expected.

At the ball held for her eighteenth birthday, I noticed our father watching her, saw his cunning, calculating mind swirling. He didn't see the child he was tricked into claiming; he saw a girl turning into a beautiful woman, surrounded by darkness and depravity yet radiating an exquisite light. Eyes flocked to her; everyone in the room took notice, and I saw all their greedy wants. There is nothing more tempting than a pure light of goodness smothered in a sea of darkness.

I kept a close eye on him from then on, monitoring his every movement, but he was watching us too. He saw the little games we started to play, how we were twisting her mind, carving out the perfect path for her to fall down the dark hole with nothing to hold on to but us. He saw everything, and he acted when I least expected it, sending her away to a boarding academy, making sure her relocation all happened underground. It took us three years to find her, but eventually, we did, and now, our dear father is rotting in a hole of his own making.

His downfall was brought on by himself; he could have avoided all of this when I offered him a deal the night before her twentieth birthday. He declined, and it was the last mistake he will ever make. He tried to create leashed monsters, but I've never been fond of being tied up. He could have remained at the top for a few more years. All he had to do was give us back what was ours. Now, he has no choice, and neither does she.

"She's here," Bastian says, the door open wide, letting in the frost-bitten air. Lightning fills the sky, illuminating Bastian's feral grin of excitement. Wet footsteps smack across the ground, getting closer and closer until two shadowed bodies fill the doorway.

Hawthorne doesn't hover, gently pushing Octavia over the thresh-old and out of the rain before scurrying back to the car. The jagged scar running down his cheek catches my eye, and I can't help the cruel grin that pulls at my lips. There are more scars littering Hawthorne's body; everyone involved in the taking of my little sister bears those scars, and this is only the beginning. The dead ones are the lucky ones. The ones left alive have learned what happens when they interfere with what is mine.

Octavia stands shivering in the doorway, her arms wrapped around her plump waist, platinum blonde, waist-length hair blowing in the wind. Her nipples are hard, showing through her thin white silk blouse, and Bastian lets out a small feral growl, biting his bottom lip as he stares.

I clear my throat in a reprimand, raising an eyebrow as he scowls. Octavia smiles widely at the two of us, her eyes sparkling with joy, but as she notices both of our eyes dropping to her chest, the smile drops. She fidgets from side to side, a frown pulling at her forehead as she bites the inside of her cheek. Her gaze drops to the floor in a demure and scared manner, and that certainly won't do. I have not waited three years for her to fear us now.

Thunder rolls through the air, lightning illuminating the moorlands once again, a storm brewing the night our dark angel returns. My polished black shoes press against the tip of her wet heels as I stand in front of her, the top of her head reaching my chest. A wave of strawberry and vanilla hits my senses, and I suppress the growl that threatens to break free. My dick hardens in my trousers, throbbing with the need to rip open her blouse and pull one of her taut nipples into my mouth, biting them until I taste blood.

But that is what Bastian would do, not me. I'm more in control of my needs. I understand that this will take a bit of time. I have the patience he does not, and that is why we agreed I would take the lead.

Slowly grazing my hands up her arms, I smirk as she shivers at my touch, keeping her gaze on the ground. Her breathing grows louder, her chest heaving, pushing her breasts forward until I feel her hardened nipples scraping against my shirt. I run my fingers across her cheek, her skin soft to the touch. She stands straighter, her spine stiff and hands clenched at her side. I place my fingers under her chin, lifting her head until her golden amber eyes meet mine.

I smirk, leaning down until my nose brushes against hers, tasting the minty freshness of her breath, her pouty lips dropping open. Her eyes widen until she stops breathing all together.

"Welcome home, little sister."

3

OCTAVIA

I can't breathe. All rational thought left my brain the moment Dorian placed his hand on my chin, lifting my head, welcoming me home. During my time away, I convinced myself that my brothers were not as sinisterly beautiful as I remembered them to be. I tried to tell myself that I built them up in my head, putting them on blood-stained pedestals because they were the only good things in my life.

I was wrong.

"Hi," I whisper, taking a step back.

Dorian pushes his jet-black hair back away from his face, creating a striking contrast against his pale skin and angular cheekbones. His appearance takes my breath away as his grey eyes meet mine. He smirks cruelly at my gasp, making him look like the sinister monster I know he can be. I'm not blind to my brother's darkness; I've never shied away from the people they are. Monsters may terrify some people, but mine make me feel alive.

He's dressed in a bespoke suit as always, handmade by the family's personal tailor. Even as a child, he wore a suit, nothing ever out of place, even while smashing someone's head in with a metal pipe. I asked him once why he always wore black and never any fun colours. He looked down at his clothes, a vicious grin on his face, and said, *"better to hide all the blood, little sister."*

It was only after he said it that I realised his clothes were damp, but not from the rain. It was from the shower of his victims' blood as they breathed their last breaths. He was thirteen years old.

Father didn't like us wearing anything colourful, but Dorian and Bastian would sneak me pretty pink and yellow dresses, always with colourful socks. I had to hide them away and only wear them when he wasn't around. A butler once caught me in a lilac dress and told my father. He beat me until I threw up and forced me to watch as he burned the dress. My brothers found me, sobbing in their bed, apologising for getting caught. They hunted down the butler the next day and gave me his fingers as a present.

There was no hiding from what I was born into; my family never shielded me from the darkness. But there was a life raft I clung to until my fingernails ripped out, and that was them.

"We've missed you, baby sis," Bastian says, wrapping his arms around me from behind, squeezing me tight.

I let out a little squeal of joy feeling him at my back, lifting my feet from the ground. My brothers enclose me in tight, one holding me too hard, the other demanding my eyes remain on him by pinching my chin in his grip. A peace settles over my soul, one I haven't felt in years. This is how it has always been with us. They have always surrounded me, giving me no space to breathe, no space to even think straight without them in the equation.

I have never felt more at peace.

Bastian chuckles, placing me back on the ground, not taking his arms from my waist. My back flush against his torso and my ass grazes against his pelvis, letting me feel the bulge inside his trousers. Immediately, my skin flushes, and I have to force myself to not push back, grinding against him. At the same time, my stomach drops, and the nausea that I felt in the car comes rearing back.

If Father sees me like this, he'll know. He'll know that my feelings for them haven't changed, that sending me to the academy did nothing but prove how much I need them. He'll send me away. I'll be ripped from them before I've even been back.

I struggle in their grasp, my ass grinding on Bastian while my breasts push harder into Dorian's chest. Pleasure rolls down my spine, my thighs shaking and underwear dampening at being trapped between them. The more I struggle, the harder they hold me, and the more turned on I become.

A hand ghosts against my bare thigh, the skirt I'm wearing not helping, leaving goosebumps in its wake. I squeal again, jolting back, stamping on Bastian's foot and head-butting Dorian's chin. They grunt and release me, each tending to their injuries.

My head flies around the entrance hall into the greeting room, searching for the scorn-filled eyes of our father or a sneaky servant peeping in the wings to report back. Thankfully, there's no one there to drag me away or report back to score points. It's just us.

I clutch my chest, breathing deeply, warding off the panic attack threatening to drown me. Bastian has moved to stand next to his twin, tilting his head to the side to examine me with a puzzled expression. He looks so cute when he does that—not that I would ever tell him.

Where Dorian is a refined evil, exuding sinister patience that could fool anyone into thinking he's the more reasonable one, Bastian is the unhinged feral twin, and he looks the part. They may have been identical when they were younger, but as they've grown, Bastian has bulked out more while Dorian stayed lean. His jet-black hair is shaved short at the sides, leaving length at the top to fall in front of his dark blue eyes. Bas got our father's eyes. He doesn't don a suit, settling for black jeans with a matching t-shirt, tattoos covering both of his arms and most of his body.

"What's up, baby sis? Are you not happy to see your big brothers?" Bas asks, his head cocked to the side. "Because we've missed you. You've all grown up."

His eyes rake my entire body from head to toe, drinking me in. My head spins, and I take a step back, wrapping my arms around my waist, forcing myself to stay in the same spot and not fling myself at them.

"Of course I have," I say with a nervous giggle. "I'm just tired; it was a long trip home. I didn't get much sleep, so I don't really feel like myself."

Dorian raises his eyebrow at my lie, giving me the look he always used to give when he could tell I was lying. Thankfully, Bastian does what he always used to do as well: he shoves Dorian's shoulder, bounding over to me, wrapping his arm around my shoulders, letting me live in my lie.

"Of course you are, pretty girl. Let's get you all tucked up in bed before the demons come out to play."

He laughs hysterically at his joke, and I roll my eyes, elbowing him in the gut, letting him lead me to my room.

"It's still not funny. This place is haunted, I swear. For two years, I had the same nightmare on the thirteenth of the month, *every* month. If that's not proof that ghost demons exist, I don't know what is."

The night after my eighteenth birthday is when the nightmares started. I would dream I woke up in my bed to find the world around me melting. Each time, I would run to find my brothers, and the demons would slowly turn up in the hallway, chasing me through the castle, laughing wickedly as I screamed. Just as they would almost catch me, my brothers would turn up and slaughter them at my feet. They would bathe me in the blood of the creatures, whispering dark promises for the future.

I would wake up in the morning to my body aching and pulsing with need, drenched in sweat. I didn't tell my brothers about the things it did to my body, watching their nightmare selves kill the things chasing me, or that I would touch myself to the thought of it when I woke. They just thought it was a horrid dream I couldn't shake, and they would tease me mercifully about it.

"Poor angel, always terrified of the demons in her sleep." Bastian smirks.

"While she should have been terrified of the monsters down the hall," Dorian whispers from behind, sending shivers across my skin.

I thought I would be stronger than this. I was determined to not let them affect me, but it's been minutes since I've been home, and it's worse than ever. Father can't see me with them; he will know in a second.

"Where is he?" I ask, not needing to voice who I'm talking about. We all know who *he* is.

Bastian's grip tightens on my shoulder, pulling me closer into his heat as we move up the stairs. Dorian's fingers run through my hair, lightly kneading my neck. "He's...away on business. He won't be back for the foreseeable future."

My head whips around to gaze at them both as they keep moving me forward. The only time he was away with no return date is when something went very wrong in the bloodline.

"Have the elders called him in? Is something changing?"

That could explain why I've been brought back. If something big is happening, a change of structure, I would be brought back into the fold to keep up the perfect image.

"Something like that, I suppose you could say," Dorian answers, keeping a straight face, but he cannot hide the gleaming hunger in his eyes. He's happy with what's happening.

"Nothing for you to worry about, pretty girl," Bastian says, bringing my attention to him, bopping me on the nose. "You're home with us now, and we'll be keeping you very, *very* close."

He grins widely, showing all teeth, making him look feral with the crazed look in his eyes. We turn off the stairs on the second level in the east wing, and they direct me down the hall. I frown in confusion, wondering where we're going.

"Change of rooms, little sister," Dorian says before I ask. "There have been a lot of changes while you were away. You'll now be in the east wing, your bedroom right next to our new one." He stops me at a door and opens it wide, revealing all my things in the bigger room.

"A few rules before we tuck you in."

Dorian twists me out of Bastian's arms, and I bristle. Whenever Dorian gives me rules, I always want to break them.

Bastian settles himself at my back, the two of them sandwiching me in again. Dorian grabs my chin, lifting my head, running his thumb along my bottom lip and making me hiss.

"Now, now, angel." He smirks. "I know you're never a fan when I implement new rules, but you will follow these with no mischief. This will be your room now. If you go anywhere, it will be with either myself or Bastian, and that includes roaming around the manor. The west dungeons and the south wing are off limits; you will go nowhere near them, and you will not like the consequences if you do."

He grips my chin tight, pulling our faces closer together, a stern, unforgiving expression on his face. "We know you like to sneak around and find whatever dirt you can, or snoop and watch us work, but that will not be tolerated now that you are back, do you understand?"

My bottom lip quivers, the harshness in his tone making my eyes water. I feel pathetic at twenty-three years old, welling up because my big brother talked to me sternly. But he's never spoken to me like this.

Even when he gave rules in the past, he was always soft with me. *Father* was the one to talk to me like this.

"Is this or is this not my home as well, Rian?" I seethe, calling him the nickname he hates. "I'm a grown fucking woman who doesn't need to be babied or tethered to your arm like a pet."

He pinches my cheeks, squeezing to the point of pain, whipping my head side to side, sneering in my face.

"No, Octavia, this place isn't your home. *We* are your home," he whispers harshly, twisting my head back to Bastian and then him. "You will do as we say. You will not move, you will not *breathe* in this place if we are not by your side. You think you know the monsters we are, but we are worse than even your mind can conjure. We've been easy on you growing up, but we do not have that luxury now. I told you things are changing, and it's time for you to embrace it."

"Embrace what?"

He keeps me in his hold, not letting go even as I try to pull myself free. I huff in frustration when he doesn't answer. His eyes bore into mine, holding me in their intensity. I can't help my gaze flickering to his lips as his tongue swipes out close to my face.

A maid squeaks in surprise, rounding the corner, finding us all pinned together. My eyes widen in horror as I try desperately to pull myself away from them. Dorian pins the servant with his stare, not dropping eye contact as he places a kiss on my forehead, slowly releasing my cheeks.

I stumble back into Bastian, flushed and flustered, running my hands over my skirt to flatten it. It's a nervous tick, as the skirt wasn't raised at all. The maid didn't interrupt a twisted intimate moment; she interrupted a brother being a confusing asshole to his sister. Only my mind is seeing it the other way because of my depraved feelings.

Bastian laughs, leaning in and kissing me on the cheek, his hand flush on my stomach. I whack him away, looking up to explain something to the maid, but she's already gone. I push Bastian away, holding the door to my new room.

"I'll stick to the new rules," I mutter, agreeing to anything if it gets me away from them and my panting thoughts.

"Good girl." Bastian grins, moving closer. "Let us tuck you in like old times," he says, about to put his foot on the threshold, but I slam the door in their faces first.

Bastian howls loudly with laughter, and I hear Dorian's quiet chuckle of amusement.

"Goodnight, little sister," they say, their voices chiming together.

"Goodnight, Bas, Rian," I shout back and then mutter under my breath, "Goodnight, big brothers."

I never call them that out loud, never dared to whisper it because of the feeling that floods me as I do. They're the words I call out at night as my hand is down my underwear, my fingers running through my cum, pushing myself over the edge again and again.

I'm sick and twisted, because I've never wanted anything more than to feel my big brothers stretching me out, filling me so deep that their cum would stay with me forever. I'm a depraved soul in a manor full of sin.

If only I could have the two sins I truly want.

4

BASTIAN

My dick is so fucking hard. I can't remember the last time it was this fucking hard. Actually, that's a lie: I totally can. It was the last time I saw my pretty girl before that bastard who calls himself our father sent her away. Three fucking years we had to wait to get her back. Three years of nothing but planning and strategizing. And blood—lots and lots of fucking blood.

Oh, that was the best part: ripping into the people who helped take her away, tearing off their fucking limbs with my bare hands and beating them bloody with them, laughing maniacally at their pleas for mercy. They were pathetic, but we don't give mercy. A quick torture session is the nicest thing you will ever get from us, and none of them deserved that. But she's here, she's back! Hopefully, my twin hasn't fucked it up.

"Bit harsh on her, weren't you?"

I'm mean, I get it. We have people stored all over that dungeon and the south wing holds our most special revenge, but I think my brother was a bit overkill.

"She needed to be told," he says, opening our bedroom door, the one right next to hers.

I push ahead, knocking him out the way, laughing as he mutters a curse, flinging myself onto our bed. "Yeah, *Rian*, but she didn't need to be told like that. I swear, if you fuck up my chances of sticking my cock in her sugar sweet pussy, I'll skin you alive."

My poor dick throbs in my jeans at the mere mention. I grab it tight, giving it a squeeze, groaning in pure agony.

He tuts at my pain, and I narrow my eyes, watching him fix his suit, keeping everything in place like the controlling bastard he is. God fucking forbid he ever looks a mess; the only time he's willing is when he's drenched in blood, lost to the hunger for violence. Once he's snapped out of it, he scrubs himself clean and fixes himself back up in a suit, looking like nothing ever happened.

"Not if I skin you alive first, little brother," he promises, sending tingles down my spine, and I shudder.

"Don't promise me a good time if you're not going to follow through. And don't call me little brother unless you want to do something about my throbbing dick," I snap, baring my teeth. "Just because you're happy to keep your five-inch wonder locked down doesn't mean I am."

Fucker knows I hate it when he calls me little brother. I'm one minute and nine seconds younger than him. Sixty-nine goddamn seconds, and the asshole never lets me forget it.

Dorian smirks, removing his tie, wrapping it tight around his fist in a way that has my cock jumping. I never do mind being his practice doll when he wants to try a different shibari position.

"It's nine inches. You know that, as you made me let you measure it and then threw a fit when you found out it's bigger than yours."

He smirks smugly, taking off his jacket, folding it over neatly on his armchair. He's obsessed with that chair; it's where he reads his favourite book. I once spilled a drink on it, so he spilled my blood, slicing my hand.

"You may be longer, but I'm thicker. Don't you forget that," I hiss, gripping my cock tighter until my balls zing with pain.

"In the skull, of course. How could I possibly forget that?" He laughs quietly, unbuttoning his shirt.

I fly off the bed, storming over to wrap my hand around his throat. His head slams against the wall with such a force, the sound echoes in the room. His pale skin turns purple with the lack of oxygen, his breathing stopped by the force of my grip. My brother doesn't struggle, doesn't try to rip my hand off his neck. He simply smirks, relaxed in my hold.

"I swear, *big brother*," I snarl. "If you've fucked things up before she's even been back one night, I will tear you apart."

My nose presses against his, spittle flying at his face. I have not waited this long for him to fuck it all up. My patience isn't like his; I've been tearing at the walls since she's been gone, my broken mind shattering even more without her.

His tongue slowly draws out, licking the spit that hit the side of his mouth. He thrusts his hips against mine, grinding his hardening cock into me. I growl in his face, an animalistic sound, as his hands shoot up, twining into my hair. He yanks me close, fusing our lips together. I bite his bottom lip until I taste blood, grinding against him, my balls aching with need. His tongue flickers out, tasting like metal, forcing its way into my mouth. I release my hold on his neck, and he inhales my breath, sucking in a lungful until we're breathing each other in as one.

I am not complete without him. His is my other half, the co-owner of our corrupted soul—being with each other is as natural as breathing. I moan into his mouth as he grabs my cock, twisting it painfully hard, giving me the pain I crave.

"I will say this once, little brother," he whispers against my lips. "She had to be told like that. She needs to push against us, to not be so protected. I know what I'm doing. She's not a delicate little princess locked in some castle. She's a dark, chained angel who needs the darkness to thrive. *We* are her darkness, and we will consume her so thoroughly, she will never find the light again."

He pops open the buttons of my jeans, pushing them halfway down my ass until my cock springs free. His nails dig into my sensitive flesh as he wraps his hand around it like it's his own, and my head falls back in pure bliss.

"I think our little sister deserves a true welcome home, don't you?"

He works his hand faster, a blade of a knife appearing in the other, cutting the seams of my top until it falls to the ground. He runs the edge of the blade over my chest that's littered with tattoos and scars, pushing deep until blood trickles down. Beads of pre-cum glisten on the head of my cock, and he releases it, swiping his fingers through the whiteness, bringing it to his lips.

"What were you thinking?" I pant, licking my lips as he tastes my cum, humming in delight.

His silver-grey eyes sparkle with that unhinged joy we share, and I know straight away what the perfect homecoming will be for our little sister.

"I think the nightmare demons need to come out to play." He grins wickedly, shredding his top, pushing me away.

I pant, adrenaline consuming my body, drowning my veins until all I can feel is the pulsing need of excitement that makes me come alive. He opens the chest at the end of our bed, producing masks and all our equipment.

"Fright night at Velka Manor has begun."

5
OCTAVIA

I t feels strange being back in the castle. I wished for nothing else every night, praying to whoever could hear me to take me home, but now that I'm back, something doesn't feel right. My skin itches, an unsettled hum vibrating through my body. I feel off, a tension filling the room, unable to be ignored.

Perhaps it's the new bedroom. My room used to be in the south wing, all alone, separate from everyone else. Father used to say it wasn't proper for a girl to share the same wing as her brothers, but he didn't seem to have a problem with Bas and Rian not only sharing a room, but a bed as well.

As I got older and more rebellious, I would scream at him about how unfair it was, earning me a slap across the face each time. He would punish me by limiting my access to the twins, keeping them so busy, I would hardly see them.

His punishment worked; it only took a few times before I never mentioned it again. Being away from them was too hard. My days would feel empty; I would wander around this giant castle, searching for them or secrets of what they were doing to feel more connected. I lost a piece of myself whenever we were apart.

My days may have been an empty void, but my nights never were. They would seek me out, silent as ghosts, wrapping their hands around mine and carrying me to their room. They would settle me in between them, most of the time covered in blood or filth, never speaking a word. They would simply hold me tight, stroking my hair, burying their faces in my neck and breathing deep. They'd sneak me out before sunrise, carrying me back to my room with a simple promise to return. And now, I'm exactly where I demanded to be for all those years: wishing I was back in the south wing.

I slam the empty cup of tea the maid brought on the bedside cabinet, burying myself deep in the thick covers on my black four-poster bed. I finally convince myself that I need to separate myself from them, to accept the tiny crumbs of just existing in the same place, and they demand that I never be apart from them. It's a dream come true and a walking nightmare all at the same time. Father might not be here now, but he'll be back. The staff will surely inform him. He will send me away for sure—or worse.

Do they not realise that? Do they not care that to be with them, I need to put as much distance between us as possible?

Of course they don't, because they don't know how sick my thoughts are—how I used to touch myself as I laid in bed between them while they were fast asleep, or how I bribed a maid to buy a selection of toys so I could use them while thinking of my twin brothers.

Technically, my family would consider me a virgin—if you believe in the concept of virginity or that it requires a fleshed cock to change that fact. I broke my hymen long ago, fucked myself with multiple dildos, screaming their names into my pillow. I might have not been with a man before, but I've had a lot of experience getting to know my body.

I'm not sure if that would count in the bloodline's eyes as breaking the rules. They believe that every woman should remain a virgin until they are matched for marriage, sold off to someone else in the family who isn't so directly related. My father called me a vile and twisted lit-tle girl for feeling the things I do for my brothers, but he and everyone else in this fucking family have a drop of blood in common. I guess mine was just too close.

My eyes become heavy, and I sink further into the pillows, feeling like I'm floating on a cloud of candyfloss. They fall shut as I drift off, laughing in my head at the hypocrisy of it all. I'm too wicked of a person to live in a castle named after the goddess of sin herself. Maybe the castle caused me to be born cursed, a rejected sinner in the house of depravity.

***

The sheer curtains on my bed turn into dripping black tar, snakes appearing from all sides, hissing, angry that I'm here. They hiss that I should leave, that I'm in the wrong place. I'm bad.

Bad

Bad

Bad

A scream gets stuck, my voice stolen as I desperately try to shout for help. I claw at my throat, nails digging into my skin, pain flaring underneath them, but it doesn't work. The world is melting away, turning into a liquified nightmare, and there's nothing I can do to stop it. It's all falling apart, and I'm stuck helpless in the carnage.

Cold sweats cover my skin, the sheets sticking to my body, wrapping around so tight that it makes it difficult to breathe. I kick my legs wildly, bucking underneath the heavy death sheet. They need to get off before I'm trapped and the sticky tar consumes me. A scream finally breaks free, the covers whipped away, and I fall thrashing to the ground on my hands and knees, landing in a puddle of red, warm liquid. Blood fills my entire floor, growing deeper and deeper, trying to suck me down. I pull my arms out, but the blood turns to slime, wet, thick, and sticky, pulling me back.

I slip, my face smacking against the wood floor, thick dark red covering my cheek. I screech, my mouth open wide, giving the blood a chance to invade me, a copper taste filling my mouth. Whispers of sick poison and bad blood taunt me. The blood speaks to me, telling me that I don't belong in the world of sinners.

Sick

Twisted

Wrong

I sob, pleading with the blood that I'll be good, that the sins plaguing my soul will stay buried.

"I promise, I'll be good. I'll be good. I won't love them that way. I'll stop. I'll be good. I'll be good." I scream each word, hiccupping between with sobs. I don't want to die. I'm finally back with them; I don't want to die yet.

The blood believes my lies, releasing my arms, slowly turning into a shallow stream instead of a flowing river coating my floor. My racing heart doesn't calm, though; it beats faster and faster, because as the blood disappears, I hear a creak. The hairs on the back of my neck raise, and I freeze in place.

"Hmmm, naughty little sinner, lying to the demons like that," a dark feral voice tuts, getting closer and closer.

"Maybe she believes the lies she tells. What a foolish little girl," a sadistic voice adds. A scratchiness in his tone sounding like nails running down a stone wall.

"No, no, no, no," I mutter, scratching my fingernails down my face, trying to claw at my eyes.

They're back. The demons of the castle are back.

Their footsteps get closer, stomping, making the floor shake. My body vibrates violently, and I grasp at the hissing snakes to keep my balance. Their monstrous feet make the world move as a snake bites my hand, causing a sharp sting. I whack the snake away, cradling my hand, my eyes welling at the pain, but my terror is drowned out when a sharp, clawed hand digs into my hair. Searing pain pulls at the roots of my hair, my head wrenched up, putting me face to face with one of the demons.

His entire face is melting like the room, dripping from his hollow eyes right down to his fanged, unnaturally large mouth. Letters on his forehead glow bright in a deep, dark red, saying 'kiss me'. I recoil away from the creature, but that only makes it laugh, bringing my face closer until I can smell the burning of flesh.

"Our angel has returned home at last, but where are your wings?"

He cocks his head to the side, and his words bring them to life. A heaviness fills my entire back right before excruciating pain. My skin tears apart, the flap of wings filling the air, white feathers falling all around us.

"There they are. Such beautiful wings. I can't wait to watch them turn black when we catch you, when you admit that you are just as dark and venomous as the demons who chase you. Our sinful angel pretending to be good," the other evil creature says, laughing cruelly.

He grips my chin, forcing me to face him in the other's grasp. Neon string has been sewn over his black void eyes, creating an X over both. The same is all over his mouth, with slits so he can speak, blood dripping down his chin. I forgot how terrifying they are.

"You know the rules, little angel. You have an hour to run through this castle and find safety," Neon demon says—not that I need to be reminded. I know this nightmare well.

"And if you don't," Kiss-Me demon continues, "then you will be all ours."

His tongue extends, licking from the bottom of my cheek all the way to my eye. I shiver, repulsed at his action and the way it makes me feel. His cold, hollow laughter echoes through my bones as he licks up the other side to match.

"Stop," I plead, hating myself and them.

"Poor little angel, always denying what she wants most," he taunts, dragging his claws on my neck and chest.

I struggle in their grasp, trying to pull away. They cackle once more, dropping me to the ground. I fling my head up to keep my eyes on them, crawling backwards, scurrying away. They laugh maniacally, never taking their gaze off me. The liquid tar moves across the room, slipping past me, crawling over the walls and ceiling, joining them, making them grow taller and taller.

"You best hurry now," Neon says, gripping Kiss-Me's shoulder, holding him in place.

Kiss-Me's melted jaw unhinges, black shadows flying out, racing in my direction as he roars, "Because we're fucking famished."

I scream my brother's names, desperate for them to get me, for them to save me. My bedroom door is already open, and I race out, pounding on their door, but they don't answer. The laughter of the demons carries into the hall, and I don't wait. I run as fast as I can, my long silk nightgown billowing in the wind that suddenly appears.

I have no direction, no thought of a place to go. My only safe place in this castle is my brothers, and I can't find them. The walls drip like everything else, making it hard to tell which way I'm going. My bare feet pad on the floor, the sound louder with each slap.

Blood flows down the hallways again, washing against my toes, making everything slippy. I've tumbled more times than I can count, the cackle of the demons always close behind. Shadows jump out, attacking as I go, whispers from the walls of the sinner who needs to be punished coming through. The castle doesn't want me here. It thinks I should have stayed away, just like my father demanded, because I'm wrong.

Sick

Sick

Sick

The castle's words get louder and louder, turning from a whisper into a thundering bellow. It tells me to leave, that I'm not wanted, but if I go, I know for sure that I will die.

"No," I scream, skidding to a halt, raging against the damn talking castle. "I will not leave. I refuse to be taken away from them again. They are mine!" I stomp my foot, raking my hands through my hair, pulling it until it feels like my skin will tear off. "Mine. Mine. Mine."

Everyone wants to take away what belongs to me. My father. The castle. The staff. The bloodline. Even my brothers. But no one can take them from me. *They* can't even take themselves from me. I will kill them before I let that happen. If the only way for me to have them is in death, then I will slaughter us all.

Movement on the wall catches my eye. My father's portrait hangs in the dripping black. He moves in it, his eyes wide with unbridled rage, staring at me the same way he did the night he took me.

"I will kill you. I will fucking kill you before you take me away again!"

I slam my entire body into the painting, trying to drag him out and bash his head into the stone, just like he did mine. I attack him in a blind fury, tearing his skin, ripping it to shreds until it sits in a pile of paper at my feet. My nails drag across the brick as the castle continues to taunt me. Black tar drips down my fingers, the castle bleeding as I try to kill it.

"There she is," a haunting voice whispers in my ear. "There's our dark angel."

My feet lift from the ground, and the demons spin me around, pinning me between them. Their bodies are so tall, all I can see is them.

"Are you ready to embrace your sin, little angel?" Neon asks, tilting my chin. His tongue extends, and he drags it over my cheek, collecting tears that have fallen.

"Are you ready to become a demon in a castle of monsters? Are you brave enough to claim them?" Kiss-Me asks, wrapping his hand around my throat from behind. "Tell us, Octavia. Say it out loud, the thing you fear most."

My breath stutters in my throat, my heart racing, about to fly out of my chest. I've never admitted it out loud, never dared to even whisper it in case prying ears were listening.

"Say it," Neon barks, his void black eyes turning silver behind his stitching, the colours swirling together until only the grey remains.

"I want them," I say, but it's not enough for the demons.

"Come on, little angel. You can do better than that. Tell us who you want," Kiss-Me whispers in my ear like a snake, trying to lure me in.

I shiver uncontrollably in their grasps, sweat dripping down my body, my nightgown sticking to my skin. I shouldn't say it. Once it's out, there's no taking it back, but I'm so tired of denying myself, so fucking tired of screaming at the demons that they're wrong.

They first appeared to me the day after my eighteenth birthday, similar to what happened tonight. They chased me through the castle, the world turning into something else, always catching me, always trying to demand the secret I hold tight inside, but I never gave it, and when I refused, they would turn wicked. I was terrified for my life until my brothers saved me, bringing me the demons' heads, bathing me in their blood, telling me it was all going to be okay.

I always deny the demons, but I'm so tired of saying no, of rejecting what I want. I'm rotten on the inside, and maybe it's time I stop pretending I'm not.

"I want my brothers. I want Dorian and Bastian living in my skin until all I can feel is them."

My darkest secret comes tumbling from my lips, and I actually watch the words floating in the air as if by magic, showing the world my shame.

"Yes," the demons hiss together, a drumming beat building. A sense of foreboding fills my veins as a change in the atmosphere thickens, and suddenly, I can't breathe. I'm gasping for air, clutching my neck where they hold me, trying to swim up through the fog.

My nightdress rips from my body, pulled by shadows of smoke, leaving me naked and vulnerable to the demons in all my truth. Neon cups my pussy painfully while Kiss-Me grabs my breasts, pinching and rolling my nipples. There's so much pain, but it's laced with pleasure, pure, euphoric, depraved pleasure.

Neon doesn't hesitate, his fingers forcing their way inside my pussy, growling deeply as I cry out. He pumps in and out, his thumb pressing a burning pressure on my clit that has my legs going weak.

"Such a sinful little slut for us," Kiss-Me hisses, licking up my neck, scraping his fangs on my pulse point.

"What a deviant dark angel you turned out to be," Neon says, black feathers falling around us. "Call out their names as I fuck your cunt. I want to hear you scream your big brothers' names as you come."

My legs buckle underneath me, a cry releases from my lips. He finds that sweet spot inside me that makes me squirt, and a blinding pleasure burns through my body. I feel my cum dripping down my legs, and I buck into the demon's hands, wanting more. Kiss-Me twists my nipples, grinding against my ass, holding me up. My arms scramble back and lock around his neck, holding tight to my nightmare.

"Bastian. Dorian," I cry. A burning heat rolls down my stomach, making my sex throb.

"Tell your big brothers how much their little sister wants them to make her scream," Kiss-Me demands, kissing my neck.

"So much," I moan, working my hips. "I want to be so good for my big brothers. I need them. I-"

A second orgasm crashes into me, and my head throws back in a silent scream. The demons don't stop until I'm a sopping wet mess, uncontrollably shaking, covering them in my cum. Kiss-Me wrenches my head back, fisting my hair as I sob. He licks my tears, humming in delight, capturing my mouth, and I don't fight him.

Neon tears us away from each other, slipping his cum-covered fingers into Kiss-Me's mouth, forcing them to the back of his throat until he gags. Saliva drips down his chin, but he doesn't fight the invasion, wrapping his lips around the fingers, sucking off my cum, not taking his eyes off me.

I'm hypnotised.

"Doesn't she taste like the best forbidden fruit?"

Neon pulls his fingers out of his mouth as Kiss-Me nods, putting them into his mouth instead. I squirm between them, keening, my pussy throbbing again, needing more...wanting more.

"Please," I beg, unable to help myself.

Neon's eyes flash, and he tips his head towards Kiss-Me. They place me on my knees between them, Neon's thumb forcing its way into my mouth.

"Keep that pretty hole open," he snarls, and I do as I'm told.

They stand together, their large cocks in their hands. I lick my lips, wanting the glistening pre-cum that rests on their tips. A slap hits my breasts, catching my hard nipples, making them burn and throb. I gasp, a shriek breaking free. Neon wraps his hand around my throat, hissing in my face.

"I told you to keep that pretty fucking mouth of yours open." He jams his fingers into my mouth again, forcing it as wide as it will go until my eyes water. I nod, mumbling an apology.

He releases me and uses the spit on his fingers as lube for his cock, working the shaft hard in a tight grip.

"I'm going to come all over your face, pretty girl," Kiss-Me hisses. "Taste my fucking cum."

A hot splash hits my face, and I stick my tongue out, catching as much as I can. He grunts, moaning deeply, and Neon grasps his shoulder, spilling his hot seed. They taste like fire and sin, burning me in the most delicious way possible.

Once they're done, they caress my face, rubbing their cum into my skin, marking me. Their touches are soft, almost loving, and I melt into them. But it only lasts a few seconds before their grip hardens, holding me in place.

A snake appears in Neon's other hand and jumps forward, sinking its small fangs into my breast. The world immediately turns to darkness, my demons laughing as I go.

"Your big brothers are going to take such good care of you, little sister. Welcome home."

6

DORIAN

O ctavia falls limp in Bastian's arms, a bit of blood bubbling where I injected her with propofol to knock her out cold. I run my thumb over it, brushing the evidence away, Bastian cradling her to his chest.

I remove that awful mask he chose to use, chucking it to the floor. We selected our masks years ago and have never changed them, wanting her to see the same monsters over and over. Mine is a standard mask you can get in most stores; I didn't want something too horrific, but Bastian's is plain revolting.

He added the kiss me on the forehead of the mask the first night we drugged her and chased her through the castle, slaughtering one of Father's spies, making it look like we were killing her demons. She cried in relief, thinking she was safe, and said she could just kiss us in a giddy high. Since then, Bastian adds kiss me on the mask each time, hoping for a kiss.

"She finally admitted it," Bastian growls, raking his gaze down her naked body, biting his bottom lip, rubbing our release into her skin.

"She did."

We've been pushing her towards the darkness for a long time, twisting her all up on the inside, making her as depraved as us. The nightmare hunts started after her eighteenth birthday. Once a month, we would slip her acid, forcing her on a trip she believed was a recurring nightmare. It started off as demons chasing her and then her big brothers coming to her rescue, her dark saviours frightening the demons away, slaughtering anyone who tried to harm her. We would change it up each time, but the one thing that stayed the same was that her brothers saved her, making us the only ones she could rely on.

Even after she *woke up,* she would come to us for comfort, and we would soothe the pain away. Our plan was working perfectly: she was falling deeper and deeper into the darkness with us as her guides—her lifeline. Her twentieth birthday was the night our plan was supposed to take its next step. Until then, we were just her protectors. We were going to plant the seed at being more, slowly poisoning her heart and warping her mind, but our father made sure that didn't happen. He sent her away, snatching her right out of our arms when we weren't paying attention.

That will never happen again.

A groan of pain rumbles from the ground, a weak and pathetic cry coming from the waste of skin at our feet. Bastian scowls in annoyance at the interruption, rearing his leg back and booting our father in the stomach. His body lifts in the air at the impact, his groan of pain turning into a sob.

Disgusting.

"I'll take Father back to the south wing. Make sure you clean her up and put her back in bed *with* a new nightgown, and leave her alone in there."

If it were up to my brother, he would have had her chained to us physically from the moment she stepped back home. But I know Octavia needs a little more pushing. She needs to come to us on her own, to give in to the sickness she's tried so desperately to fight. I want full surrender, not an unwilling captive.

"You take the fun out of everything." Bastian snaps, giving Father one last kick.

I click my fingers, and a flurry of people jump out from the shadows, waiting for my order. Two of them grab my father by his arms and start dragging him back to his room while the others clean up the bloody mess my dark angel made.

I follow behind the ones that have my father whistling a tune. Octavia was magnificent in her attack, a feral, bloody demon as she raked her nails down his face, slamming his head into the wall repeatedly. I'm not sure if she realised it was him while she was tripping. She could have been seeing anything, but I have a feeling she saw some extension of him.

We pass multiple staff as we go, cleaning up after us. The hunts can get rather messy, but the ones who were here before she left will be used to it. They are the ones who aren't shaking in fear or retching as they work. It takes a lot of work to create this, a lot of clean-up. It's why we only ever did it while Father was away, with staff who are loyal to me.

The men dragging my father chain him back up into the room where he will enjoy his limited stay, securing him to the bed. It's Octavia's old bed, in her old room. I thought it would be fitting for her to kill him here when the time is right.

"You won't get away with this," father croaks, pulling weakly at his restraints. My gaze snaps to the men, and they rush out of the room, closing the door behind them. I slowly walk towards my father, tsking as I shake my head.

"I believe I'm already getting away with this."

I never liked my father, and love is completely out of the question. We don't love in the bloodline, but I did respect him, how he ran his part of the organisation. My family is the shadow in the night, the monsters crime lords are terrified of. We don't just control the underworld from the shadows; we control everything: CEOs, banks, politicians, gangsters, even royalty. No one knows about us, only the myth. My father excelled in what he did, but he made the mistake of trying to take what's mine.

"The elders won't approve. They'll find out I'm missing when I don't check in, and the first ones they'll come for are you and your brother. How could you betray the bloodline like this? All for some little who-"

"I would be very careful about finishing that sentence," I hiss.

He's acting desperate, trying to make out like the elders won't approve when we both know they would. The bloodline runs on depraved power; it's the only thing they respect. If an outsider were to do this, then he would be right: the entire bloodline would be out for revenge and blood. But his own sons doing this, someone a part of the bloodline? They won't bat an eye. They will see it as weak. There's no coming back from weakness, and he knows it.

"They won't accept a marriage between the three of you. They think you're too closely related. They will marry Octavia off to someone else, and you will lose her again. That's why I sent her away in the first place, to save you from being cast out by the family for being with her. I knew after you asked me for her that you wouldn't be able to resist her poison. She's just like her mother; she will ruin you. I only wanted to protect you from that." He tries a different tactic, trying to hold in the panic from his gaze.

"If you release me, we will forget this ever happened. I'll tell the elders that Lucinda was already pregnant before we wed, that Octavia isn't mine. She's still part of the bloodline and far enough for you to be together. They will let you keep her, and I will help. I'll sacrifice my standing. I promise, son. Think about it. You know this would be the right decision."

I laugh cruelly at his comical, pathetic version of what happened. This man truly believes me to be a fool.

"I know why you sent her away. I saw your beady eyes on her at the ball. You truly saw her for the woman she turned into. But when you found her diary and saw how much she wanted us, your poor warped ego couldn't handle it. You've never been good at second place, but that's where you always find yourself. Your marriages, the bloodline, your sons. There's always someone better."

His face turns bright red, his bloody, broken body shaking with rage. "I taught you everything you know. You are nothing compared to me. I run this bloodline!"

The elders run this bloodline. He's just the figurehead in charge, but not anymore.

"Have fun screaming at the walls. I'm sure you can convince them you run this bloodline while chained to a bright pink bed." I cackle as he bellows in rage, the chains rattling as he thrashes.

"They will never accept the three of you together! Never!"

I grip the door, cocking my head to the side, frowning deeply. "Then they die too. Enjoy your last days, Father. The countdown begins."

7

OCTAVIA

My head is pounding. It feels like someone is running a drill through my skull, my mouth bone dry. My tongue sticks to the roof of it, and a cold sweat shivers down my spine. I hate the morning after a nightmare; I always feel like I have an epic hangover. They stopped when I was at the academy. Of course, they reappeared when I returned to the castle.

I flush as I remember the nightmare, or the last part of the nightmare, at least. It's always such a haze, bits and pieces flashing into my mind. But the demons that chase me stay with me, like they're burned into my skin, no matter what.

My brothers didn't come and save me last night. They didn't brutally destroy the creatures that toyed with me. They were nowhere to be found, and the demons captured me. Their game turned into a different kind, a more twisted kind, one where they toyed with my body, making me scream my brother's names. It was completely fucked up...and I loved it.

Even as my body is screaming out in pain, my pussy throbs between my legs, my nipples hardening, remembering their touch. I cup my breasts in both hands, pinching my nipples like the Kiss-Me demon did. My breath stutters between my lips, a small whimper escaping at the sensitivity. I must have been touching myself in my nightmare, because my nipples feel sore to the touch—used.

I drop my hand between my legs, pulling my nightgown up to expose myself. I'm already wet, wanting the touch I envisioned. My teeth sink into my bottom lip as I hold in a small moan, placing the pad of my two fingers on my clit, slowly moving in a small circle. My hips flex, rolling with the movement, warmth spreading through my core. I increase the pressure and speed, my back arching off the bed of its own accord. I'm as sensitive down there as I am on my nipples.

It doesn't take much for the burning pleasure to make my toes curl. I pinch my nipple harder, doing the same to my clit, rolling it between my fingers. My orgasm bursts through me, small but still so fucking nice. I arch my back more, a silent cry releasing from my lips. I don't stop until my legs shake and my limbs turn to liquid.

Thankfully, I don't squirt this time. It was too small of an orgasm with no internal stimulation, so at least I won't have to flush with embarrassment when one of the maids comes to change the sheets. That has happened a few times over the years.

I fling off the cover, going over to the ensuite bathroom in desperate need of a bath to soak my body. It's the only way I'll start to feel better. That and some orange juice. I used to crawl into bed with Bastian and Dorian as well, but that option is completely off limits now. No more squishing between the two of them and letting their warmth bring me peace after a nightmare. I can't take that risk.

As the door cracks open, a frightening growl is released, and I pause, freezing in place. My eyes dart around the room quickly, taking everything in. There are no melting walls, no snakes or shadows jumping out. Everything is exactly how it's supposed to be. I'm not in a nightmare at all, but it sounds like one of the demons is in my bathroom.

Another growl echoes, different from the first, only to turn into a moan. I take a small peek inside, making sure not to be seen, holding my breath. My shoulders drop, and I let out a sigh of relief seeing Bastian's and Dorian's bare backs with a towel wrapped around their waist. I also notice another door on the opposite side, one that must go into their room.

Fan-fucking-tastic. I'm sharing a bathroom with them. Great. Just great.

It wasn't like living in the same place with them wasn't going to be hard enough. Now I have the utterly pussy throbbing chance of running into them naked in the bathroom? I swear, the devil is trying everything possible to lure me into her darkness and trap me there forever. Twisted bitch.

It's not *not* working.

My brothers groan again, a feral hiss coming from their lips at the same time. I step forward just a tiny bit to see what they're doing, only to check that they're okay and nothing else. I'm their little sister; it would make sense that I want to make sure they're okay, right?

Shit, even the lies I'm telling myself are no longer believable.

Bastian twists, slamming his ass against the vanity sinks, and drops his towel to the floor. My hands fly up to my mouth, covering my gasp, my eyes widening. His hand tightly grips his cock, working the entire shaft, the head of his cock painted with pre-cum, making the four metal balls in the shape of a cross around the top glisten.

I've never seen a piercing like that. He hisses again, rubbing his palm over them, his head thrown back in pleasure. He's gotten more tattoos since the last time I saw him, and one of them stands out like a neon sign. Over the top of his throbbing cock is a red tattoo that says 'kiss me'. I want to crawl on my hands and knees and do exactly that: open my mouth wide and beg with my eyes for him to fuck my throat until I have tears streaming down my face. I want him so far back, he's choking me until I can no longer breathe, but my lips can touch that tattoo and do exactly what it says.

I know I should move, that I should quietly shut the door and pretend I haven't seen him, but he's not alone in the bathroom. My other brother, his twin, is there with him, and I'm desperate to see what he's doing.

Dorian lounges on the chaise lounge next to the clawfoot tub as he leisurely works his cock, watching Bastian with a deep intensity. His eyes blaze with depraved pleasure, a cruel smirk on his lips. The towel he was wearing is spread underneath him, his pale body shimmering with water droplets. His wet hair is brushed back, showcasing his angular jaw, and he has never appeared more like a god of darkness than he does in this moment.

Bastian's legs shakes as he fucks his hand, cursing between his teeth, staring at Dorian like he's about to kill him. The sound of flesh slapping has my pussy tingling, wanting me to touch it and join them in this fucked up moment...but I can't. Fear paralyses me; I'm afraid that any movement will make them notice me, and if they notice me, they might stop.

Bastian snarls at Dorian, his eyes speaking even if his lips don't. I'm not sure what he's saying or what he means, but Dorian does.

"Hold it," he orders, his smirk growing as Bastian curses at him.

"Bastard!"

He keeps fucking his hand roughly, a pained look flashing across his face, his hips stuttering as he does as our brother ordered.

Dorian keeps working his cock at a leisurely pace, but the more Bastian curses at him, the more I see little twitches in his body. His legs go stiff, spine straightening, and his grip tightens.

"Oh, fuck. Dorian!"

Bastian moans loudly, and my eyes fly in his direction, worried I missed his release. His other hand is cupping his balls, but he hasn't come yet.

"Hold it," Dorian barks, releasing a toe curl growl as he spills all over his chiselled stomach, decorating it in with his cum.

Bastian storms forward, towering over his twin, watching with deep fascination at every drop that expels from Dorian's cock. He licks his lips, punching his hips, fucking his hand harder.

"Now," Dorian orders, and Bastian snarls, shooting his load all over his brother's chest, their releases mixing together.

Dorian's hand shoots up, catching Bastian's chin before he's finished. "Get on your knees and clean up our mess, *little brother*."

My brain stops working. I unfreeze and pinch myself all over my arm—this can't be reality. Surely, I've fucking died and ended up in some sort of twisted hell, because this doesn't happen. It shouldn't happen. I've fallen down a rabbit hole and found myself in a nightmare land where everything that shouldn't be done is being done, where right is wrong and wrong is right. But if I am, I don't want to ever escape.

Bastian crashes to his knees, his tattooed hands gripping Dorian's thighs, digging his fingers into his flesh until he snarls. Bas chuckles, leaning forward, dragging his tongue through their mess, humming in delight.

I gasp again, but this time, I can't catch it, and it echoes into the bathroom. Dorian grips Bastian's head, keeping him there, but his slowly rises. I duck out the way before he can see me, running over to the bed, chucking myself under the duvet, shutting my eyes. My heart pounds in my chest, my sex throbbing so painfully, it actually aches. I'm not sure if I want them to come in and catch me knowing what they were just doing or hope that they had no idea.

Seconds tick by, and I don't hear anyone come into the room. I wait until it feels like long enough and peek my head above the cover. My room is empty, and the door to the bathroom still slightly cracked, just as I left it. I creep over to it again to find the bathroom empty and the door to theirs on the other side closed.

They didn't see me.

That's a good thing. It's for the best. Just because they like to... *have fun*...with each other doesn't mean they would feel the same way towards me.

It... a... fuck!

It is so fucking confusing. I was staying away from them because I thought they would think I was sick and disgusting for wanting them the way I do, but after what I just witnessed, could I be wrong?

8

BASTIAN

I grin wickedly, glancing up at Dorian, catching his smirk. We both hear her breathy gasp as I gather up our salty cum, sensually moving my tongue along Dorian's muscles. Only a few seconds later, we hear her footsteps rushing off with a panicked yelp. I rip my head from Dorian's grasp; the fucker took full advantage of our audience to boss me around.

He opens his mouth to say something, and I use that opportunity to grip his cheeks, spitting the cum on my tongue straight into his mouth. If I have to taste us together, so does he.

"Next time, you can be the one on your knees like a little bitch. Instead of consuming my cum, I'll force my dick down your throat until you choke on it."

We played a game of slash, stab, or spear to see who would be getting on their knees. We both select a weapon, and the first to draw blood wins. Unfortunately for me, I lost. The bastard got me in the back of the neck with a small dagger, a weapon he *didn't* select. He picked the butcher knife knowing that it was my favourite and I would be pinning over it while he used it. He took advantage of my obsession with the pretty weapon and cheated. But the fucker *did* draw blood, and he had the dagger on him before he started, so I suppose it was fair.

The taste of us together doesn't bother me that much. It's not like I haven't tasted my own cum before. It was a first tasting Dorian's, although it wasn't much different, possibly a little muskier. Still, it got us where we needed to be, pushing us a step closer to our end goal. Little sister has had a pure taste of forbidden sin, saw our depraved souls in action. She's seen us kill before, but she needed more.

Dorian stands, gripping my wrist, removing my hand from his cheeks. His eyes stay locked with mine, holding his tongue out, letting me see the creamy whiteness before slowly pulling back and swallowing.

Fuck... Okay, that was hot. I see what baby sis sees in us: we're temptation wrapped up in a poison-laced bow.

"Next time, win the game, and you'll get your wish, little brother." He smirks, patting me on the cheek, walking naked into our bedroom.

My gaze slides to the other door, the one to her room still left open a crack. I bet she's laying in bed touching herself. I bet if I went in there right now, her legs would fall open eagerly, her pussy begging me to sink deep inside, desperate for me to fuck her until she's screaming my name. I would consume her until all she could see is me.

"Bastian," Dorian calls, and I hear the order in his tone.

I pull my eyes reluctantly from her door, narrowing mine at him as he raises an eyebrow. Huffing in annoyance, I stomp into the room, barging my shoulder into his and aggressively digging out some clothes.

Dorian gives a hum of approval, shutting the door, sliding over the lock before he gets dressed. I've never been bothered about him being in charge; he possesses the right temperament for it. I got all our aggression, and he got all our patience. Together, we make a great team. If you took away one of us, it would fall apart. We cover each other's weaknesses, and leadership has never been my strength. Still,

I'm getting a bit fed up with all this waiting. When it comes to her, we're equal. When it comes to her, I would kill my twin if he thought he could place me second.

I growl, kicking the drawer closed with my booted foot, burning frustration running through me. I need to either fuck or kill something, and seeing as I can't fuck anything at the moment, I suppose I'll have to settle for killing.

Dorian grabs my shoulder, holding me in place as I try to storm out of the room. I have a knife held up to his throat in a blink of an eye, pushing it deep until blood trickles against the black metal. Dorian sighs, but he doesn't let go of my arm or pull away from the knife.

"Tonight," he says, one singular word, but it has my anger disappearing in a second.

"Tonight?" I ask, raising an eyebrow, pushing the knife a little harder.

"Yes, brother. Tonight." He rolls his eyes, shaking his head, making more blood flow freely. "I believe our show has given her another push into our darkness."

Dark, electric energy buzzes through my veins, thundering electricity lighting me up from the inside. Tonight, it will finally happen: I will get to have her beneath me as I feed the ravaged demon that's been clawing for a taste of her flesh. She has always been mine, and tonight, she will finally realise it.

"Go kill something before you end up fucking everything in sight." Dorian chuckles, staring into my bloodthirsty eyes and down to my waist, where my dick is rock hard.

I flick my knife away, grabbing my brother on the cheeks, smacking a wet kiss on his lips. "You handsome fucker. Sometimes it's hard to remember why I shouldn't kill you, and just when I think to do it, you remind me why I shouldn't." I wink, slapping him on the ass, cackling while he scowls.

"I share the sentiment, brother, but right now, I'm more inclined to kill you for that slap."

I lick his blood off the knife, skipping away, poking my tongue out over my shoulder. I slam into a butler in the hallway, making him drop a tray of food. His startled, wide eyes tell me someone was listening when they shouldn't be.

"Ooh, someone has been naughty!" My unhinged smile widens, and the butler stumbles away, falling back onto the wall.

"Please, sir." He holds up his hands, crouching into a ball.

Bad luck for him but fantastic for me. I thought I was going to have to make the trek *all* the way down to the dungeons and select one of the many people there to kill. Sometimes having them all there just gives me too much choice.

Should I slaughter the man who assisted in hiding where Octavia was taken? Do I torture Octavia's old nanny who used to scowled her when she wanted to spend all her time with us, saying it wasn't right? Or do I burn the staff members who used to tattle on her to Father?

It makes me feel like a child in a weapon shop; how am I supposed to choose just one? But now, I don't have to, all because this lovely butler has made the choice easy.

"Oh, Jeeves. I'm sorry to say today is going to be your last day here. Time to meet your demons."

I launch at him, grabbing his hair, dragging him down the hall. He kicks and screams, begging for mercy, but there is no mercy in the manor of sin. I cackle madly, slamming him into the wall as we go.

He cries all the way down to the dungeon; it would have been much more preferable if he screamed. I like it when they scream. I'm not a fan of tears, especially when they choke on their own snot and it bubbles out of their nose. Ugh, turns my fucking stomach.

The chains rattle as I secure them around Alfred's wrist, and he doesn't even fight it, already accepting what's happening, his head hanging onto his chest.

"Way to take all the fun out of it, Barnaby," I snap, slamming my knife into his thigh.

He cries again, whimpering like a little bitch, and I tut, rolling my eyes, tilting my head, pointing a thumb towards the other guy. "Fucking buzzkill. Am I right, Chad?"

Chad doesn't answer; instead, he hangs there limply, rats nibbling at his toes. I only painted them yesterday, goddamn it. Pink for Octavia, as it's her favourite colour. I've been practising painting fingers and toes so I'll be perfect when she wants her nails done. She won't need to go to a salon and have a stranger touch her. No, I'll do it. I've been getting fantastic—lots of people to practise on down here.

"Oh, my God. Oh my God," Jarvis mumbles, vomit flying out of his mouth, soaking down his shirt. "He's dead. Aaron is dead."

Huh, that's his name. Definitely looks more like a Chad or a Brad.

"I ran out of dead bodies to practise my nail art on," I say defensively, grabbing the knife out of his leg and slamming it into his stomach when he carries on staring at me like I'm crazy.

"It's all for her, you know? I need to be everything I can for her. She gives us so much peace; she understands us. I need to make sure I'm perfect for her." My voice drops to a whisper, and I go into the corner, grabbing the nail kitt and bring over a chair and a stool.

"Stay still," I mutter, placing Smithers' feet on the stool, taking off his sock and shoes.

He pleas for something, trying to make conversation, but I grab a nail file, jamming it into his leg until he shuts up and I can tune him out. Today, I want to paint a daisy on the big toe like I saw on the video online.

I've bought every colour nail polish you can imagine for my pretty girl. Until she reached sixteen, Father restricted her to using only clear polish or French-tip, and after that, it was only red. Octavia hates the colour red—always has, probably from seeing too much blood as a kid.

I protected her from seeing it as much as I could, more than Dorian. She was my princess, something soft and sweet, much too kind for this life. I didn't want the bloodline to do to her what it did to us. From the day we took our first breath, Dorian and I have been ruined, our souls stained. She deserved more.

"I tried the whole dating game once. Went out on my own, attended balls without my brother, let our father introduce me to prospecting partners, but all I felt was an empty void with each one."

He grunts, a whimper escaping, and I know he's fascinated by my tale.

"I know it's hard to believe I wanted someone else, was willing to leave my twin, but I was. There was this hollow hole inside me searching for something. I just wanted to be loved, to be needed, but no one was ever a match. They would get jealous over Dorian or moan if I cancelled plans because Octavia needed me. They didn't get that they would never come first compared to them."

I slip some tissue between his toes, gently blowing on the nail-varnish so it dries. Igor sobs, shaking his head, and I completely get him. This colour does not go with his skin tone, but this isn't about him.

"No matter who I dated, who I found underneath me, they didn't fill the emptiness. Only *they* have ever filled it so thoroughly, and it wasn't until I stopped fighting it that I realised I never needed anyone else. I was complete with them, and they will always be more than enough."

I grin, looking at his wiggling toes. The flowers look perfect. She is going to love them!

"Let me tell you a secret," I whisper, jumping up and pulling him closer. "I love them, fully love them with my entire being. We're not supposed to love. It's a weakness the bloodline doesn't tolerate, but them and especially her, I love with a power that feels like it's about to burst from within."

He's speechless, totally speechless, staring at me wide eyed with his mouth hanging open. I hope Octavia doesn't have this same reaction when I tell her, because I do plan to tell her.

"Say something then. Do you think she won't enjoy hearing me tell her?" I snap, slapping him round the face.

A disgusting snot bubble blows from his nose, making my stomach turn. He stutters, pleading like a blubbering idiot, totally ignoring my question.

"Oh, forget it. I'll ask someone else. You've already smudged your toes."

I grab the nail file out of his leg and stick it straight into his throat and through his windpipe. Guess I'll be selecting one from the body dungeon after all.

9

OCTAVIA

"I said I'm fine, Rian," I snap, my cheeks burning red, a hot flush trickling down my spine where he touched me, pressing his palm to my lower back, asking if I needed anything.

All day he's done this. Little touches here and there, crowding me in when there was no need, reaching for things across me, pulling my chair right next to his when I refused to sit on his lap.

I'm in hell. My own personal hell.

Dorian smirks as I run my palms across my extremely short, black and white tartan skirt, my thick thighs out on display. It was the only thing hanging in my wardrobe this morning, along with a tight, black, long-sleeved top, black Mary Jane shoes, and pastel pink knee-length socks. My outfit of the day.

I've never been able to select my clothing. Each morning, I would wake to only one being in the wardrobe, hand selected and confirmed by my father. My brothers would sometimes sneak me different things to wear, but never a full outfit, and this had to be them. Father would never have allowed for me to be in a skirt this short or have no freaking underwear on. No, that's not true. They provided me with a bra, a sheer black one that clasps in the front and has a lot of fabric missing. My large breasts threatening to spill out.

Three years ago, I would have flushed with embarrassment, thinking they were playing a joke on me, but after seeing them in the bathroom, watching them together, I'm flushed for a completely different reason. My sex has been pulsing all day, hoping they might not think my feelings for them are as fucked up as I believe, that maybe this outfit is a sign they could see me as something other than their little sister.

"I really need to speak to the maids about the outfit choice they left this morning," Dorian says, snapping me out of my thoughts. His gaze lands on my hands tugging my skirt down. He purses his lips, raising an eyebrow.

Oh, well, there goes that thought.

"This wasn't your selection?" I whisper, tugging harder now to make sure I'm concealed.

Of course, he didn't select it. Devil, I'm such an idiot. It was probably a new maid who panicked without my father there and handed me something old that doesn't fit my body as it used to.

Dorian doesn't answer, simply sweeping his gaze up my body and returning his attention to his computer, dismissing me. I huff in annoyance and embarrassment, crossing my arms across my chest. He types away, humming in displeasure a few times. I've already grown bored, sneaking glances to see what he's doing, but none of it makes sense. I want to get up and explore the castle, maybe go see the cooks and see if they have any sweet treats on hand.

No point in trying, seeing as I'm not allowed to be anywhere in this place without one of my brothers by my side. One is fully concentrated on work while the other is fuck knows where. I haven't seen Bastian all day. I bet I could have convinced him to do something fun, unlike Dorian.

"Stop fidgeting," Dorian mutters, slapping my bare thigh and clamping his hand around it.

I suck in a sharp breath at his burning touch, wetness immediately pooling between my thighs again. He swipes his thumb back and forth over my flesh, leaving a trail of goosebumps down my skin. If his hand was an inch higher, he could feel how wet I am. Just a single stroke higher, and my secret would be out.

I stop moving, grasping the arms of the chair, digging my nails in to stop myself from hitching my hips forward, wanting him to feel what he does to me. My chest rises as I take slow and steady breaths. My nipples harden, and there's no hiding them in this sheer bra, no padding to protect them from being seen.

"Good girl," Dorian whispers, giving my thigh a praising squeeze.

I hold my breath waiting for him to let go, closing my eyes tight, willing for his touch to release me even as I secretly wish for him not to. His thumb skates up my thigh, pushing back the fabric of my skirt, and I can feel my heartbeat in my ears drowning out everything else. I try to hold in my shiver, to not show what I'm feeling, but it's too late. A whimper of pleasure spills from my lips, my head falling back, his thumb continuing to rise.

I don't dare open my eyes, afraid of the expression on his face or for the chance that this might stop. His breath hits my cheek, the warmth of his lips dangerously close to my skin. All the air leaves my lungs, leaving me drowning in a fog of sin.

"Dear, sweet sister. Do you really think I would be letting you roam the castle in this outfit if I didn't specifically select it for you?" He darkly chuckles, brushing his lips over the shell of my ear.

My thighs quiver, my whole body shaking. I suck in a gasp of air, my eyes springing open to find he's moved in front of me. The heat in his gaze burns my soul, the wickedness in his smirk making my skin flush.

"Dorian." I breathe his name like a dark prayer, begging him with everything I have without actually saying anything.

His smirk turns into a wide, sinister grin, stretching his lips so much, his features become manic. "Is that what you really want to call me, little sister?"

I choke on my own spit, spluttering in his face, but he doesn't move. I shake my head, but I'm not sure if it's an answer to his question or a denial that I want to use any other name.

He knows. How the fuck does he know?

"Say it," he whispers seductively, moving his hand from my thigh and running his thumb over my bottom lip. My tongue moves on its own, catching his flesh, tasting him for the first time. He hisses at the contact, placing his thumb on my tongue, forcing it to stay hanging while his fingers capture my chin.

"Say it."

The demand has my eyes wanting to roll to the back of my head, white hot pleasure moving through my entire body. I move my jaw, working up the courage to say what I want, what I've been dying to say for years as he removes his thumb. He keeps hold of my chin, placing his nose on mine, breathing in my breaths. The tension is so thick, it could choke us both.

"Big br-"

A throat clears, interrupting us. I tug my head away from Dorian, ripping it from his grip and try to scoot my body away from him in the chair.

"Sir," a male voice calls.

Dorian's eyes turn murderous, the control he always holds slipping away. His muscles shake as he holds himself in place, towering above me, watching with a snarl as I look away from him. This side of him doesn't frighten me. I've seen him lose control only a few times, but it never scares me. No, it intoxicates me.

"What?" Dorian answers in a calm voice that doesn't betray the rage simmering below the surface.

The butler clears his throat again, obviously nervous. He should be. A rage-filled Dorian speaking calmly is never a good thing. Bastian would have bashed the guy's head against a wall for interrupting him, or possibly just yelled until he made the person piss themselves, but Dorian will hold onto this. He will wait until you think it's safe, formulating the perfect revenge for the slight he perceived, and then he will act.

"The...uh... Dinner is about to be served, sir. I was told you wanted to be notified and fetched as soon as it was."

Just like that, the anger flips off. He straightens up, holding out a hand for me to take, a small smile pulling at his lips. "Ah, perfect. Of course. Thank you, Quincy."

Quincy breathes a sigh of relief, but I cringe, grasping Dorian's outstretched hand, letting him pull me to my feet. We walk past the butler, and he holds the door open, smiling at us. Dorian smiles back, nodding his head in thanks, but I shake mine slowly, making the butler frown with a puzzled expression. Hopefully, one of the staff warns him. Just because he was doing as instructed doesn't mean he's off Dorian's list.

I wish knowing he was like this made me hate him. Sometimes, I wish knowing how brutal my brothers were could stop my feelings for them. There's nothing morally grey about them: their souls are pitch black, shrouded in toxic darkness and stained with blood, but I've already been infected with their poison long ago. There's no saving me, and if I had the choice, I wouldn't want to be.

10

OCTAVIA

D orian and I don't talk the entire way down to the dining room. He keeps my hand clasped in his the entire way, never uttering a word or looking at me. My lip is sore from the amount I've bitten it on the way down, wanting to say something but not sure what.

The table is already laid out as we take our assigned seats: me on my own on one side while Bastian and Dorian sit opposite, our father at the head as far away from us as he can get. Except now, it's just me and Dorian. He's already taking bites out of the chicken the chefs have prepared, and I'm pushing mine around the plate, my appetite non-existent.

How on Earth can I sit here and eat after what happened? How does he know that I want him, that I've wanted to utter the words *big brother* while he touched me? Have I been that obvious? Did Father tell him?

"Everything okay, Octavia?" Dorian asks, rudely interrupting my mental breakdown.

My cutlery crashes against the plate as I drop them, taking a big swig of wine. If Father was here, my *unwomanly* behaviour would appal him. Women in this family were only good for marrying off and breeding. God forbid we have our own minds or goals or achievements.

Dorian smirks, raising his glass of neat whiskey to his lips, amused as a trickle of red wine seeps from the side of my mouth, running down my chin. I slam the glass down, scowling back as I catch the droplet with my thumb before sucking it off. My own smirk grows seeing his grip around the glass tighten, his throat bobbing, eyes locked on my mouth.

"Is that the type of game you want to play?" he asks, raising an eyebrow, a motion I copy, but I falter as he adds, "Little sister."

I run my tongue across my lip, contemplating. Do I take the risk? This could all be an elaborate plan of our father's to find out if I've truly gotten rid of my twisted affliction. Dorian and Bastian have always protected me from him, always been on my side, but what if he disclosed to them why I left, and they felt repulsed? What if all of this is a ploy? They might cast me aside, and I could end up losing them for good.

"Really? This is the love you two show your sibling? Starting dinner and not even waiting for me!" Bastian bellows, slamming the door open.

I gasp in my seat, my hands flying to my face at the sight of him. Blood covers his bare chest and arms, across his face. I'm flying out of my chair towards him before my brain has even caught up, ploughing into his body, not caring about the sticky substance that covers him.

"Bas," I cry, patting him down, trying to find the wound. "Are you okay? What happened?"

There've been plenty of times Bas stumbled into my room with one wound or another, needing to be patched up. Dorian is sprouting a fresh wound on his neck at this moment. I've been patching up my brothers since I was six years old, Bas more than Rian. They still have jagged scars from the botched job I used to do, but I got better, and they would have no one else do it once I started.

He wraps his arms around me, stopping me from checking on him, breathing deeply into my hair as he chuckles at my struggle.

"Seriously, Bastian. Stop fucking around and show me where you're hurt," I snap, stomping my foot. He always said a hug from me stops the pain, but it doesn't stop his body from bleeding.

"Aww. Is my baby sis worried about her big brother?"

He holds me tighter, squishing my face into his blood, making me feel the wet warmth that coats him. Dorian's chuckle reaches us, doing nothing to help at all, both of them unbothered by a possible life-threatening wound. I swear, these two are the most deranged people in the entire fucking world.

"Yes," I seethe. "Now let me see the wound before I kick you in the dick, *big brother*!"

Bastian stills, and I huff a piece of hair out of my face, pulling back in relief that he's going to let me check him, but he doesn't let me go. The room fills with tension, bubbling over my skin, making my stomach flip and my heart pound. It's exactly the same as it was in the office with Rian, but this time, it feels more. More alive. More dangerous. My skin prickles, and shivers run down my body.

"Say it again," Bastian growls, keeping me flush to his chest.

It takes two seconds for me to understand what he means, but as I do, I freeze just as much as he does. I called him big brother. I haven't done that in years, not after I started looking at them differently and that name took on another meaning.

"You have three seconds to say that again, Octavia, or so fucking help me..." Bastian leaves the threat open ended, and I wonder what he will do if I don't say it. It almost makes me not want to.

"I said, *let me see the wound before I kick you in the dick*."

I straighten my spine, preparing myself for what I'm about to do. Either way, there's no going back. I'll have my answer. Bas snarls an unholy noise, fisting his hand into my hair, yanking my head back. The anger on his face takes my breath away, and I whisper, "Big brother."

His lips crash into mine, his tongue demanding entrance that I willingly give. Pleasure explodes all around me, his touch everything I dreamed it would be. His hands grasp my bare ass, lifting me as my legs go weak, not once stopping his demanding kiss. I forget the blood and the possible wound and fall into him.

Bastian kisses like he's trying to consume me, leaving no room to breathe or even think about anything outside of him. We crash into the table, and I barely feel pain at the dishes smashing around us.

"Do you know how long I've waited for you to call me that, little sister?" Bastian growls against my lips, fisting my shirt as I sit on top of the table.

I shake my head, eyes wide, mouth open. He rips my shirt apart, revealing the black sheer bra, setting my skin on fire. He moans at the sight, cupping my breasts in his palms, tweaking my nipples.

"Fuck! You always did have great taste, brother." He bends his head, taking one of my nipples into his mouth, running his tongue across it over the fabric. I cry out, arching my back, pushing my breast further against his mouth, wanting more.

"I only enjoy the finest things. You know that, little brother," Dorian says, sitting closer to us, lounging back and watching. Bastian growls at the name, clamping his teeth around my nipple, making me scream as Dorian smirks knowingly.

"Tell our little sister how long you've wanted to stretch her cunt on your cock, little brother," he taunts again, and Bas clamps down harder, making me hiss.

"Years," Bastian growls around my nipple, staring up at me through hooded eyes. "I've wanted to stretch, taste, fuck, and claim your sweet fucking pussy for years."

I keen as he slips two fingers into my pussy while he says it, not waiting for permission or asking if I want him to. He takes my pussy like it belongs to him, touching me like there would be no reason not to.

"And how long have you been lying to us, Octavia?" Dorian asks, dragging my attention away from Basian's fingers stretching me.

"What?" I stutter on a moan, my eyes rolling to the back of my head. Bastian crashes to his knees, pushing my skirt to my waist, exposing my sex. He grips my thigh, fingers digging into my soft flesh, pushing it open and running his tongue up my clit, sending sparks of pleasure through me.

"I asked you a question, little sister. Pay attention," Dorian barks, and my head snaps up.

Bastian chuckles, sucking my clit into his mouth as my hips buck against him, my head swimming, trying to focus on Dorian.

"I...I never lied to you," I mutter, grasping Bastian's hair, keeping him in place.

Dorian tuts, slowly rising from his chair and moving to our side. "I think you *have* lied to us. You've been pretending for years that you didn't want us, that your sweet cunt hasn't been desperate for us. You've been rejecting us at every turn." He cups my cheek, shaking his head in sorrow.

I gasp in rage and in pleasure as Bastian adds another finger, finding my g-spot, focusing solely on it as he sucks my clit perfectly.

"I've never rejected you. I didn't even know you felt the same way. You shouldn't feel this way... I shouldn't... It's wrong... Twisted," I cry even as I thrust onto Bastian's hand.

"Yes, but that makes you like it more, doesn't it? The sick twisted-ness of wanting your big brothers to fuck you. It makes it that much more fucking delicious, doesn't it?"

Dorian's lips are on mine as he speaks. I desperately want him to kiss me, to feel his tongue against mine while I fuck Bastian's face. One touch of his lips, and I'll come. My orgasm is building so tightly in my body, I'm seconds away from it.

My head nods and shakes, two parts of me battling out inside, neither the winner. I want this so badly, it hurts. He's right: the forbidden-ness of it makes their touch so much more electric, but I've spent years denying myself. I can't help the denial whispering out.

"No."

Dorian steps away as Bastian gets up from between my legs, stealing the orgasm that was just about to happen. "No, I didn't mean it. I-"

I cry, my body shaking, everything in overdrive.

Dorian sighs heavily, shaking his head as he walks away.

"Wait," I shout, making him stop and turn, but nothing more comes out.

"Don't worry, Octavia. We won't touch you again—not unless you can admit it. When you do, I want you crawling on your knees begging for your big brother's cock. I want to hear all the ways you've fantasised about us, *every* single one. And if you can't..."

He doesn't finish the sentence, shrugging his shoulders as he walks to the door.

"And if I can't, what?" I ask, tears running down my face, overly exposed everywhere, the orgasm denial making me a jumbled mess.

Dorian turns back and smirks cruelly, giving me a dismissive glance. "Then I suppose you'll make someone in the organisation a perfect, timid wife."

A burning fury runs down my spine, and I see red, grabbing the first thing I can reach to fling at him. Black glass smashes against the wall by his retreating head, narrowly missing the bastard.

"Fuck you!"

I'm seething. He always promised that, no matter what, they would never let Father marry me off. No matter what he said or did, Dorian and Bastian promised it would never happen.

Bastian stands in the middle of the room, scowling at the empty doorway Dorian just went through. His body is racked with tension, his muscles stiff, hands clenching at his sides. The blood on his body is all smeared, decorating my chest, thighs, and face now as well.

Dorian calls his name from the hall, but he doesn't go to him. Instead, Bastian storms over to me, grasping my face in his hands and forcing his lips on mine. His fingers find my clit, and he rubs in furious circles, winding me up quickly.

"Fall into the darkness with us, little sister," he whispers. "Come on my fucking fingers and fall into the dark for me."

I scream against his lips, wrapping my arms around his neck. White hot pleasure pools in my stomach, my release dripping down my legs as they shake.

"Yes," he hisses, working my clit faster, making me squirt for the first time with no penetration. "That's it. Come all over my fucking hand."

I pull frantically at his neck, scratching and tugging his hair until his lips are back on mine. I take everything he willingly gives, unsure if it's the first and last time.

"You are mine, Octavia. I claimed you as you were taking your first fucking breath, and you claimed me. Embrace the darkness, little sister. The light burns sinners, and you are the most sinful of them all."

He releases me suddenly and walks away. Dorian stands at the doorway glaring at us both before stomping off, and Bastian smirks over his shoulder, sending me a wink and a kiss. I stumble to my feet, needing to get to him.

"Bas, your wound."

I need to stitch him up or it won't heal, but he keeps on walking away, shaking his head.

"Not my blood, pretty girl."

I halt in place, frowning, and he cackles, sending me another wink.

"Don't wait too long to beg. You know how much of a psycho our brother is. The punishments will be fun for us; not sure how you will feel about it, though." He blows me another kiss, his laughter echoing in the halls, and my stomach drops.

II

DORIAN

B astian huffs, slamming the door and stomping out of the shower, rattling around in his drawers, hunting for something to wear. I can feel his eyes burning into my skin as I read in my armchair. He hasn't spoken since we left the dining hall, since he defied our agreement to leave our little Octavia wanting if she didn't admit she wanted us—although he played straight into my plan, the one he doesn't know about.

I thought it may be too soon for Octavia to fully admit her desires out loud, but I pushed it sooner because I knew Bastian needed it. I hoped for the best, but it didn't surprise me. My brother did. He always follows me, going along with whatever I deem fit. I assumed he would follow me out and leave her an unsatisfied, shaking mess but, to my pleasant surprise, he didn't.

Bastian has always handled her more softly, treating her like a princess. He never pushes her, gives in to her every whim, and always waits for me to give the go ahead, holding himself back, afraid to scare her off.

"Is there something you want to say?"

I place the book on my chest, raising an eyebrow, waiting for him to blow. Containing emotions has never been one of his strengths.

"Yes, there's something I want to say, *big brother*," he spits, charging forward, ripping the book from my hands. "How could you say that?

How could you even think of giving her away to someone else when she is mine...*ours*?"

Ah, yes, that's what has him all in a tizzy most. The poor, unexpecting staff all scattered when he stormed out the dining room. They were most likely terrified they would end up his next victim. I told him I might threaten that, but it looks like he's forgotten in his fury.

"Answer me," he barks, wrapping his hand around my throat. His favoured move. He always goes for the choke, probably trauma from how many times our father choked us as a child. It's one reason I can withstand it for a long length of time. It also hardens my cock, but I won't analyse that too deeply.

Our bedroom door slams open, and Octavia stands in the doorway, her hair and clothes dishevelled in that freshly fucked way, fury burning in her gaze. She didn't bother to put her top back on, only dressed in her bra and skirt with those cute as fuck socks. Blood stains her delicious plush flesh and hair, making her look like a bloodthirsty angel seeking violence.

My cock hardens even more, Bastian's grip becoming even tighter, and I lean into it. His muscles shake with restraint as he licks his lips hungrily, hope in his eyes that she's come to beg.

Her step into the room falters for a second, her gaze finding us and taking in the scene. For a second, the fight leaves her eyes, and worry filters into my stomach, but she soon shakes her head, squeezing her eyes closed for a second before she marches forward.

Bastian lets go of my throat, and I suck in a deep breath. He stands up straight, bouncing on the balls of his feet with eagerness. I opt for the opposite, reclining back in the armchair, picking up my book again, pretending to read.

"Come to beg so soon? That didn't take you long."

Bastian hisses at me the same time she does, fuelled by anger, and I'm their target. It's adorable, like two pissed off kittens.

"Don't flatter yourself, Rian," she snaps, using the nickname she always called me as a child. I let her believe the name annoyed me, but I've always enjoyed it when she was angry, her darkness bubbling under the surface.

Our little angel has been slowly filling with poison to be just like us. I ensured it. When she gives in to her anger and lets it out, she can be just as vicious as us. My little sister shows it now, as quick as lightning, by throwing my book across the room and holding a carving knife to my throat.

Bastian takes a step forward—either to help me or to help her, I'm not sure which—but I hold up my hand to halt him. "It's okay. Octavia is all hiss and no bite. I'm fine."

Octavia's hand shakes, her pupils blown, a deep dark need for vengeance taking over. It looks so delicious. My dick throbs in my trousers, my bare chest begging her to slice me. And she does.

The knife presses harder against my skin, so sharp that it cuts like butter, and I feel my blood slipping down it.

"How's that for all hiss?" she whispers in my face, her lips so close to mine. I push myself onto the knife, cutting deeper so I can bite her bottom lip, dragging it into my mouth for a taste of her fury.

She hisses, grabbing the top of my hair with her free hand, yanking my head back, pulling her lip free, but she doesn't press the knife harder.

"Don't fucking touch me." She shakes my head, moving the knife and slashing me across my chest. "Don't you dare fucking touch me after going back on your promises, threatening to marry me off like a prized cow. I'm not an item to be sold. I will never be sent away or removed ever again, even by you," she snarls, her upper lip curling.

I cock my head, running my gaze over her body, drinking her in. "And what will you do about it if I decide that's what's best?"

I stand, towering over her, watching as she takes a small step back. "Tell me, Octavia. What will you do?" I whisper.

She doesn't think, not even for a second, and slams the knife into my thigh, twisting it.

"I will slaughter any fucker in this castle who tries to send me away," she whispers, pure, unhinged madness sparkling in her eyes.

There she is.

I grunt as she twists the knife in my thigh one more time before letting go, storming out the way she came, the stomp of her shoes booming with each step.

"Oh, and I also want a credit card and a laptop so I can order my own fucking clothes for once," she shouts over her shoulder before gripping the door and slamming it.

I fall back in my chair as she leaves with that last demand, laughing with joy. Bastian stands with his mouth hanging open, his head swivelling to the door and back to me.

"That, dear brother, is why I threatened her with the marriage."

She needed a little more pushing, that was all, and look at what a glorious outcome we got. Bastian's stunned expression morphs into a more sinister one, the wires in his brain connecting. She will never fully accept her wants and needs if we're always shielding her from *our* darkness. She thinks she has seen it all, but she has no idea. She doesn't need to be protected from it; she needs to be lured in and consumed by it, to embrace it on her own. My way isn't gentle; I'm not her knight in shining armour protecting her from all the bad things. I *am* the bad thing, and I will feed my soul into her until she is as damned as us.

"You twisted bastard. I could fucking kiss you." Bastian smirks, eyeing the knife in my leg, cocking his head. "How hard are you right now?"

I groan, grabbing my cock in a strangled grip. "Painfully."

I slip my trousers down my ass carefully to avoid the knife still sticking out of my leg so it doesn't pull out. She didn't hit anything serious; we taught her all the places to stab a body, so she knew what she was doing. I will need to get it stitched up soon, but first, I need to take care of my throbbing need.

"Spit," I order, needing the warped feeling of my brother's saliva running down my cock before I come from our little sister stabbing me.

Bastian grins, sauntering over, towering above, letting his spit trickle down onto my wanting cock. I moan as it hits, my head falling back as I rub it around my shaft. He stays above me the entire time, his eyes fixated on my movements, his own cock hard. He takes hold of the knife, and I growl, working my hand faster. He twists it just like she did, leaning forward.

"I can't wait to watch our little sister on her hands and knees, begging us to fuck her," he whispers, "her body covered in blood after she's slaughtered our father."

I buck into my hand, lifting my thigh to take more of the pain from the knife, my balls growing tight, the image flashing through my mind.

"I'll watch you take her first, big brother, and then I will make her sit on my face, tasting you on her, cleaning your cum from her as she explodes. I bet you will taste so fucking sweet together."

I hiss as I come, white ropes hitting my chest, mixing with the blood still there. Bastian mixes his fingers through both and sucks them clean, growling deep. I shiver as the last drop leaves me, and I relax back in the chair, my thigh burning in pain, adding to my afterglow. Bastian pats my chest over my wound, and I jolt forward, hissing at him as he laughs hysterically.

"I'll go get the medic for you. I doubt Octavia will be stitching you up, seeing as she's the one who did it. Lucky bastard. Why didn't I get cut?" He frowns, his emotions changing like a flip of a switch.

He mutters to himself as he walks out, complaining that she didn't use the knife on him and how he needs to up his game, be more of an asshole. My twin's moods change like no one I've ever met. Minutes before, he was ready to choke me for being an asshole, but I adore him for it. Without him, I wouldn't be half as sane as I am. Without them, I doubt there would be anything I ever cared for in this life.

No one else means anything to me. Everyone is disposable when their usefulness ends. I don't enjoy the killing like Bastian does; it's a means to an end and does nothing for me. Mental games are my favourite, twisting someone up until they start to doubt their own sanity is what I live for. I may use mental games on my siblings, but that is always for a greater good, to get us where we need to be. They have nothing to fear from me. Others cannot say the same.

My phone pings with a message I've been waiting for, and I smile seeing his name flash across the screen. My grandfather is joining us in the castle in two weeks' time to go over another lead that went dry in search of my father. That has been a fun game I've been playing, acting the sad grandson desperately trying to help his grandfather find his son. That will be coming to an end just in time, the outcome undecided for the moment. It all depends on how much Octavia can stomach. If I have it my way, she's going to be out for blood.

12

OCTAVIA

"Gotcha again, pretty girl. You're going to have to do better than that."

Bas grabs me around my stomach, cupping a good handful of my breast, spinning me around.

"Have I told you yet how fucking hot you look in this dress?" he whispers biting my neck, making me gasp. He drops me to my feet, dashing away again before I can smack him around his thick head.

It's a Bastian babysitting day today because I'm still not allowed to be in my own home without one of them by my side. Bas has been the one with me the most since I stormed into their bedroom and pushed a knife into Rian. I'm not sure if Dorian is angry with me for doing it or not. He has only *watched* me two days out of seven, giving me access to a credit card and laptop, but he hasn't spoken to me. He only gives me heated glances when he sees me in one of my new outfits. It's been a dream being able to buy clothes designed for a curvy body, so all my items actually fit me properly now. I went with my style for once, getting sweet, cute outfits that are revealing at the same time.

Bastian hasn't been silent about it. Every day, I put on at least three different outfits in order to tempt my brothers into taking me instead of making me beg. So far, it hasn't worked, but Bas is close to breaking, I can tell.

The first day he watched me by himself, he was a complete asshole, acting just like Dorian. I was seriously about to find another knife and stab *him* in the thigh this time, but he cracked when I changed into a short, white, frilly dress, going back to his hyper crazy self.

He likes me in white, I've figured out. It's why when I realised he was watching me today, I selected a long, white silk dress with thin straps that barely contains my breasts, form-fitting to show off all my dips and curves, a high slit on the side that goes almost to my hip. Of course, I couldn't wear any underwear with it. It would have shown through, and that would be a massive fashion don't. It wasn't anything to do with the way he growled and punched a wall, blooding his knuckles.

I complained to my big brother how bored I was stuck in the castle with nothing fun to do, pouted that I wanted to play a game while running my hand up my thigh, trying desperately to think of one. He had the brilliant idea of playing hide and seek tag like when we were little, but instead of getting a sweet or teddy if I won, I told him I wanted him to get on his hands and knees and eat my pussy.

The way his lips turned up in a feral grin had my thighs clamping together and my heart racing. I knew getting Bastian to crack would be the easiest...or so I thought.

I'm a hot and sweaty mess, panting and out of breath for all the wrong reasons, because every time I get close, the fucker evades me. My bare feet hurt, and I'm getting serious thigh chafing running through this fucking castle. What I thought would be a fun game has turned into a goddamn nightmare, almost as bad as my actual nightmares. At least in the last one, I got off. With this, I'm having no such luck.

I race after him again, the competitive drive bubbling under my skin more than my desperate need to come. I guess wanting to fuck my brother still doesn't stop that need to compete with him in everything.

Slightly fucked up, but damn, a competitive sibling streak is on the low end of my fucked-up tree.

I rush past some of the staff, ignoring their looks of confusion or furrowed brows of worry. One opens their mouth to say something, a gasp in their breath and pure fear on their face. I must be close. Bas would have probably put the fear of the devil in them, thinking he was running at *them*, not away from me. I hurry my steps, going up the staircase, turning down the hallway.

Resting for a moment, I take slow breaths, trying to stay silent to hear him. I slowly tiptoe down the hall, my feet sinking into the plush carpet. A low, agonising groan fills the air, sending goosebumps onto my skin. It's not Bastian; I would know his grunt of pain anywhere. Freezing on the spot, I twist around, taking in where I am. It's my old hallway, the one I'm forbidden from, and the moans of pain are coming from my old bedroom.

My head flings back and forth, searching for anyone around, but it's empty, not a soul in sight. Dorian's threat of punishment rattles around in my brain, but the temptation here forces the worry out.

My hand is on the doorknob before I can blink, the rush of adrenaline filling my veins, the thought of being caught making my clit throb. Doing the wrong thing always gives me such a thrill, even when I don't want it to.

The bedroom in front of me is bare, blood staining the walls, a foul scent drifting from within as soon as I open the door. My once spotless carpet is now ruined with unspeakable fluids. I gag, trying to hold my breath, covering my mouth with my hand. The only thing in this room is a bed, and on top of it lies a brutally beaten man with a swollen face, half healed nail marks tracking down his bare chest, burns all over his arms and legs.

I gasp, bringing his attention to me. He shakes his head, blinking his eyes rapidly.

"Octavia?" he rasps, his voice changed from what I remembered. "Tavi, is that really you?"

I always hated it when he called me Tavi. He only ever used it around company, trying to make it sound like an endearment, but not once did he ever say it without a silent sneer when no one was watching.

"Father," I mutter, stepping into the room.

Dorian and Bastian said he was called away by the bloodline, that they didn't know when he would be returning. There's no way he turned back up in the week and a bit I've been home. Some of his wounds look old, and this room reeks. He must have been here for months.

"Thank God you're here. Your brothers have gone mad, Tavi. They fooled me and locked me up to take over the bloodline. We have to save them before anyone finds out. If the Elders get any word of this, it will be all our heads."

He lunges forward, rattling the chains that bind him to the bed. I keep moving forward, my body on autopilot. He breathes sighs of relief, and he fixates his gaze on me as if all his prayers have been answered. What a fool.

"You're not the one who called me home," I mutter to myself, but he believes I'm talking to him.

"No. No. I did, Tavi. I was in the middle of arranging everything to bring you back when they attacked me. I was so distracted without you here that I got sloppy and weak. I missed you so much, daughter. I couldn't function without you, and your brothers took advantage of that for their own gain." He rushes his words, shaking his head furiously. "I was wrong to send you away, I know that now. Your brothers poisoned you, twisted you with their sick, disgusting ways. You were innocent in all this, my sweet Tavi."

His chains give him enough reach that his hand grabs mine, yanking me closer to the bed. His foul smell emitting has bile creeping up into my mouth, but I swallow it down. My father pleads with his gaze, giving me the most loving look he ever has.

"They did this on purpose," he whispers. "They knew I would feel like a piece of me was missing with you gone. They knew it would weaken me to send my only daughter away. I acted out of protective anger, but I was wrong, so wrong. We need to get out of here. Set me free so we can go to the Elders. I can't stand the thought that they might hurt you because of your brothers. I love you so much, Tavi."

He has actual tears welling in his eyes, full fucking tears. My father is good. He's really fucking good.

"You love me, Father? Really?" I whisper, making my voice shake, gripping his hand.

He holds mine back tight, nodding his head eagerly, hope shining in his eyes. His lips pull almost into a sinister smile, but he manages to pull it back, softening it. "Of course I love you. You're my little girl, my sweet baby."

I stare up at the ceiling, shaking my head, biting my lip. "I've always wished for you to say that. I can't believe you care for me so much. I'm just... I'm so overwhelmed."

His grip bites at my flesh, tension filling his jaw as I make a show of fake tears, prolonging it for as long as I can.

"I know, and I'm sorry I never showed it before," he says through his teeth, breathing harshly. "But we really need to go before anyone finds out you're here. They leave the keys to the chains in a box right under the bed."

I bet that was Dorian's idea. My father is in the room with literally the key to his escape, sleeping on top of it not even three feet away from him, but he can't get to it ever. So fucking twisted.

"You really love me, Father? Truly?"

His shoulders tense, his neck straining as he tries not to sneer, burning alive with fury on the inside. "Yes, Octavia. I already said I lov-"

"You really love me even though I'm so fucking desperate to sink to my knees and open my mouth wide for my big brothers?" I cut him off, yanking him forward with all my strength. He yelps in pain, his arm pulling out from its socket, the chain twisting it at an odd angle.

"Do you really love the twisted, sick whore you birthed? The one literally panting at the idea that her big brothers did this for her? My pussy is fucking soaked knowing they did this to you." I bend, placing my face in front of his, his vile breath making my skin shiver. "Because they did this for me. Your torture, your death, is all for me, and as soon as I leave, I'm going to get down on my hands and knees and beg them to fuck me," I whisper.

His face turns so many shades of red and purple, I think he's about to burst all his blood vessels. His body shakes, making my arm rattle. I give another tug, making him cry in pain before letting him go.

"This is all your own making. What I feel for them is all your own fucking making. You gave us no love, no kindness. You left the three of us together, closing us off from the real world with only each other to hold on to. You used them, tried to turn them into your personal monsters, and gave them nothing but blood. You isolated me, gave me no friends, no other family apart from them. What did you think would happen?"

We were all homeschooled. The only activities my brothers got were assignments for the bloodline, and I had none. The only time

I ever saw people were at annual balls, and I was only allowed to attend bloodline weddings when I hit eighteen. He gave me no one but them and gave them no peace or love but what they got from me. He moulded us into what we are, and he punished me for it.

"I can't wait until they skin you alive," I hiss.

"You filthy fucking whore! I never fucking loved you. I wish I killed you the day you slipped out of your mother's cunt. You're not my fucking daughter!" he rages, thrashing violently on the bed. "I will kill you. I will kill you and those boys. You're nothing to them. You're not even-"

"Having a pleasant family reunion without us?" Dorian says, entering the room, cutting our father off.

Father opens his mouth, spit dripping down his chin as he snarls, but he doesn't get a chance to say anything else. Bastian walks in holding some weird type of pliers, a gag with a metal circle, and a knife.

"I always said you talked too much, daddy dearest. I think now is the time to fix that."

Bastian storms over to our father, and he screams, shaking his head, rambling something I don't quite catch. Bas drops the stuff on the bed and wraps his hand around his throat, strapping on a gag that forces his jaw wide open.

I feel Dorian's warmth on my back before he reaches me, his arm coming across my chest, holding my chin still, forcing me to watch what's about to happen. I don't fight him. He didn't need to force me; nothing would stop me from watching this.

Bas uses the pliers to hold father's tongue as he thrashes, shaking his head to get him off, but nothing is stopping my big brother. Bastian's eyes are as wide as our father's, shining in pure excitement, watching terror consume his victim's gaze. He cuts through the tongue slowly, making every second count. Father wails in agony, the fight leaving his body quickly; he passes out when Bas is only halfway done, slumping in the bed.

Bastian leaves the gag on him, chucking the rest to the floor, including the tongue. Blood is splattered on his face and shirt as he walks towards us, licking it off the side of his mouth, his pupils blown. He crowds my front, Dorian staying at my back, caging me in.

"We were supposed to be playing a game, pretty girl. You broke more than one rule by coming in here," he husks, running his bloody hand across my plump stomach, staining my white dress.

He bunches the fabric, transfixed by the contrast of the red against the white. He can't stop staring at it, yanking me a little closer, unable to stop himself. "What do you think we should do with you?"

"Fuck me," I whisper, shaking in their hold.

Bastian's gaze snaps up to mine. Dorian's grip on my jaw tightens, and he tips my head. Neither say anything, and I know what they're waiting for.

"Please, big brothers. Fuck me. I want you. I want you both so fucking bad, it hurts." My voice shakes and my thighs tremble. I told our father the truth: my pussy was drenched when I realised what they had done to him for me.

Bastian groans, gripping my hips in a painful grasp, grinding his hard cock on my stomach. Dorian chuckles coldly against my neck, laying soft kisses up my throat. "Such a good little sister," he whispers, running his tongue across my cheek.

Bastian cups my pussy, holding it in a firm grip, his eyes darkening with mischief. My head falls back into Dorian's chest, fully intending to fuck them in this disgusting smelling room where our father lays mutilated on the bed not six feet from where we stand.

"But you broke one of the rules, Octavia," Dorian tuts, and I can feel his smile on my flesh. "You need to be punished first."

My heart pounds frantically in my chest, ice cold fear trickling down my spine, at odds with the white-hot pleasure that consumes my sex. Bastian feels my excitement, cupping me harder, moving the fabric out of the way to fully feel it.

"Such a sick, twisted whore," he hisses. "You were fucking made for us."

Bastian's lips capture mine while Dorian's stays on my throat. I hum in delight, his tongue demanding entrance, and I taste him mixed with the blood of our father. If being sane takes all this away, then I don't want it. I want to bathe in the darkness with my brothers, let them consume me until I see nothing but them, and all they have is me.

13

BASTIAN

I have the most perfect view in the entire fucking universe. Seriously, I don't think I've seen anything better. Actually, it could be a little better if Dorian hurried up instead of being a damn perfectionist in *everything* he does.

"Good pussy. Pretty pussy," I coo, lifting my hand, gently tickling the soft blonde curls on Octavia's cunt. She jumps and then shivers, trying to close legs, though that's impossible with her tied up like a pretty present.

"Are you going to stay there the entire time instead of helping?" Dorian huffs, slapping Octavia's thigh to keep her from wriggling, twisting the red silk ties in an intricate pattern all over her body.

I tilt my head up from between her legs as she stands, raising an eyebrow at him. He's completely fixated on his last few sections, biting his bottom lip. There's no way he wants me to help. I'm not into the pretty ropes so much; the bondage I like, but how long it's taken him to do it is such a bore. Luckily, I have the best view in the house to keep me occupied.

"You'd get annoyed and try to stab me if I even attempted to help," I scoff, hooking a finger into the silk tie that leads the entire way down Octavia's slit, a few knots added along the way to increase the pressure. One of them rubs against her clit as I do so, and she cries out, legs buckling. I twist my head, biting her calf to make her cry louder.

Dorian kicks me in the side, smacking her across the ass. "Would you stop making her move? I'm almost done."

"Killjoy." I pout, springing up to my feet, taking the temptation away.

He rolls his eyes but finishes hooking the last of the ties, giving them a good pull to make sure everything is safe. Our little sister looks like a piece of art, blood red silk ties twisted in intricate knots, crisscrossing all over her stomach, back, arms and thighs. Her hands are tied in front of her in a prayer against her chest, a long tie going to the ceiling to keep her steady, her legs locked in place by a bar ankle restraint.

"Perfection," Dorian whispers, and I agree with him.

Her head whips around as we stand, watching. Her breathing is erratic, chest heaving. "Dorian? Bastian?"

Pretty girl is blindfolded with noise cancelling earbuds in. Her senses are cut off, part of Dorian's punishment. He circles her like a predator hunting its prey, letting his fingers touch her now and then, making her jump.

His first smack is quick as lightning, catching her on the ass cheek, and she jolts forward, her body automatically pulling away, but she has nowhere to go. He doesn't delay the next few; the smacks get harder—her thighs, her breasts, and lastly, her drenched pussy.

She screams as he hits her between the legs again, a beautiful cry falling from her lips. Her head tilts back as she moans, Dorian pulling on the rope rubbing against her clit.

He keeps at it until she's a shaking mess, calling out our names in a needy voice that makes my dick throb. She whimpers in his face, nodding, leaning forward for a kiss, but he grasps her face, digging his fingers into her cheeks, coldly laughing before he tuts.

"Not yet, little angel. We're only getting started on your punishment," he says, even though she can't hear him.

He runs his tongue over the seam of her pouty lips, taking delight in denying her, smacking her pussy one last time.

"Your turn." Dorian smirks, letting her go and handing me the equipment I asked for. He saunters to the side, removing his tie and shirt before dropping into a plush black chair.

I circle Octavia as my fingers brush across her neck, moving her plait to the side and removing her earbuds. Dorian grunts, but I ignore him. He had his fun tying her up, and now, it's my turn.

"Hello, little sister," I whisper in her ear.

She gasps, pulling against the restraints, twisting her head towards me even though her blindfold is still on. "Bastian?"

She breathes against my lips, and I can't help flicking my tongue out for a taste.

"You look beautiful all tied up for your big brothers. Are you nervous, pretty girl?"

She licks her lips, nodding, swallowing hard, shivering in the room. Dorian specifically put the air-con on, wanting her nipples painfully hard.

"Do we scare you, Octavia?"

I step to her other side, dragging my fingers across her naked back. She rocks on the balls of her feet as I give a little push, and she moans when the knot on the rope rubs against her clit. I bet that little bundle of nerves is in overdrive. That was the first thing Dorian did, wanting her to be an overstimulated, whimpering mess before we even started.

"Yes," she whispers, catching her breath. I grab a handful of her plump ass, groaning at the touch of her flesh on mine. "But...but not in a bad way. I...I like the...fear."

I wrap my hand around her front, pulling her roughly against me so she can feel my cock grinding against her ass. I pull the rope, basking at her whimpering in my arms.

"Your fear is intoxicating, little sister," I growl in her ear. "I'm going to shatter you into a thousand pieces and collect them all for myself. You are mine, Octavia. You've always been mine and now, you're going to scream for me."

I flick on the vibrator, placing it against the knot that rests on her clit. She cries out immediately, her hips grinding, desperate for relief. I don't make her wait for it, not prolonging any second, wanting to watch her fall into oblivion.

"Thank you. Thank you. Thank you," she chants, blissfully ignorant of what's coming. Dorian likes to prolong things, to draw them out, but my favourite is not stopping. She won't be thanking me soon.

"Tell your big brother how good he's making you feel, little sister," Dorian orders, trousers unbuttoned, his hand wrapped around his shaft.

"So good. You make me feel so good, big brother. Make me come. Please, make me come."

I chuckle against her neck, sinking my teeth into her flesh, lapping up the blood that fills my mouth as I pierce her skin, shivers running down my spine as I listen to her scream. "Be careful what you wish for, pretty girl. This is a punishment, after all."

"W...w...what?"

My chuckle turns into a wicked laugh as she comes, squirting all over my hand. I give her no time to calm down or breathe, turning up the vibrator, pushing it harder onto her clit and pulling the rope at the same time. She thrashes frantically, screaming at the top of her lungs, but she's powerless.

"This is the first of many. Come for me again, little sister. Now."

"Oh my God. I can't stop. Bastian. *Bas*."

The bind attached to the ceiling shakes, pulling tighter, holding her up as her knees buckle. Cum covers my hand, and I'm desperate for a taste. Dorian is there before I even ask, holding the vibrator for a moment.

I lick my palm, growling at her flavour. His eyes darken, and I hold two fingers out to him. He doesn't hesitate sucking them into his mouth, his tongue catching every drop.

"You taste like the most sinful meal, but if I hear any other name from your lips, I will show you why they call me the viper of the bloodline," Dorian hisses against her lips. "Now taste yourself on my tongue."

He hands the vibrator back to me, slowly kissing her, feeding her his tongue inch by inch as she sucks. I flip it up another notch, another sweet scream ripping from her throat. Dorian drops to his knees, staring up at the both of us, and opens his mouth. I shake the vibrator, and he plunges his fingers into her pussy. He starts with only two fingers but quickly works, adding another and another, forcing her to stretch for him.

"Are you going to take my entire hand, angel? Do you want me to fist your sweet fucking cunt?"

She nods her head frantically, pushing her hips forward. "Yes. Yes... Oh fuck, yes!"

She screams as his entire hand forces its way inside. He fucks her with his fist, and I turn the vibrator to full strength, her scream turning into something wild. Dorian pulls his hand out, and she squirts everywhere as he opens his mouth, letting it drench him.

"Fuck," I grunt, rubbing the vibrating across Octavia's clit faster, prolonging her orgasm.

I've died and gone to hell. This is fucking amazing.

14

OCTAVIA

"**P**lease. *Please*."

A sob racks up in my chest, the blindfold that covers my eyes soaked to my face from tears and sweat. Dorian and Bastian have me clasped between them, easing the restraints holding me. I can't stand, my legs no longer working. I'm completely worn out, but my pussy doesn't seem to get the memo.

I've lost count of the number of times I've come. I don't know how long this has been going on or even what day it is. There is only them. Nothing else. I can't think, can hardly speak, but I *need* something.

"What is it, baby? What do you need?" Bastian whispers softly in my ear, acting like a sweet protector when he's actually the devil. He's been relentless in my punishment. I thought Dorian would be the worst, but Bastian has exceeded my expectations.

"Please," I husk, my voice destroyed from screaming. "I...I can't... I need...big brother."

I whine, wiggling between them, not making sense, but nothing makes sense anymore. Only them.

"That's enough, Bastian."

Bastian matches my whine, but the vibrator on my clit stops, and I sigh in relief. I could worship at their feet. Anything they wanted would be theirs. My soul, my life, my death—I would give it all to them for finally stopping.

"We don't want your death," Bastian chuckles as Dorian says, "But we will take everything else."

Shit, did I say all that out loud?

"Yes, you did. Now close your eyes for me," Dorian orders, and I do as I'm told.

His fingers skims across my sweaty cheeks, tugging at the blindfold that has stuck to my face. He pulls it off, and I keep my eyes shut.

"That's my good girl."

Dorian lays a kiss on each of my eyelids, the touch so sweet and soft, it has a lump forming in my throat. "Keep them closed for me and stand still while we work. Bastian has you," he whispers, and I feel Bastian's arms looping around my waist, taking my weight.

The binds holding me snap away from my body, the sound of a knife cutting through rope filling the air. After each cut, Dorian rubs my flesh, his sweet lips trailing kisses as he goes. I whine in Bastian's arms, trying to pull away from their touch and chasing it at the same time.

"You did so well for us, baby," Bastian praises softly in my ear. "Your pussy is a work of fucking art. I can't wait to lick you clean once our big brother fills you up."

I squirm in his grip, rubbing myself all over him. Dorian hisses against my thigh, removing the ankle lock. My sorely abused sex throbs with need at the mental image, and I pant, unable to help myself.

"Do you like the thought of me licking his cum out of you? My mouth filled with both of your releases as you suffocate me? I want you to sit on my fucking face until I pass out. I want your scent burned into my senses as the devil tries to drag me to hell."

Bas slips his hand between my legs, cupping me hard, two fingers slipping inside, feeling how much he's turning me on. He hisses, dragging his tongue up my cheek and sinking his teeth into my skin.

"You're so fucking drenched. Such a beautiful, broken mess for us." He twists my head, and rests his lips on mine, not kissing me but breathing in my air.

"I love you, Octavia. You are what keeps my heart beating."

I suck in a deep breath, his breath, my eyes flying open even though Dorian told me to keep them closed. The light in the room burns, making me hiss and whimper in pain, but I force them to stay open.

We don't say love in this family; it's not a word we use at all. No one in this goddamn bloodline loves the other because we have it literally beat into us that love is a weakness. I have loved my brothers all my life, but I've never told them that because...because we don't say the word.

"You...you just said..." I stutter, unable to form the sentence.

I spent a month with my grandfather when I was ten years old to be taught what it meant to be in this bloodline. I experienced beatings and torture for a week, which ingrained in me the belief that love destroys and bloodline loyalty is the only thing that matters. I didn't need the beatings, to be honest; Dorian and Bastian had ingrained into me that we could never say the 'L' word no matter how much we care for each other. They had six months with Grandfather when they were ten.

"Bas..." I whisper, a lump forming in my throat.

Bas gulps hard, a vulnerability in his gaze that I have *never* seen before. It takes my fucking breath away, my heart stuttering in my chest. The world falls away; I don't even feel Dorian anymore or the weakness in my body. It's just the two of us.

"You said you loved me."

He nods his head slowly, licking his lips, touching mine at the same time. "I would break all the rules for you, Octavia. I wouldn't just kill for you—I would fucking die for you. You are the only reason I stay alive." He turns me to face him, cupping my cheeks. "I love you. I love you. I love you. I promise that, after today, you will never go another moment without me saying those three words to you. You are mine, pretty girl, until death do we part."

His lips consume me, and I fall into the kiss, letting it fill my entire being. My heart is pounding so hard in my chest, I fear it might break. I'm terrified that this might be a dream or a memory, that any moment, I'll snap back into reality and lose this...*them*.

"I love you, Bastian. There's never been a time where I haven't."

He pulls back, a glorious smile stretching across his face, still a bit too wide to look entirely sane. I smile back, my eyes filling with tears at the joy on his face. I try to tell him again, to say it three more times like he did, but I lose my breath. Hands clasp my ass from behind, lifting me up, only to let me fall back on a hard, throbbing cock sinking inside me.

"Now that you two have said the forbidden words, it's my turn," Dorian rasps in my ear.

He forces my legs up, wrapping them around Bastian, letting him hold them up. I fall back onto his chest, his arms coming around to grab my breasts, his cock sliding through my slit, making me keen. There's no resistance in my body, and he slides in so effortlessly, his hips snapping against my ass.

"Your cunt feels so fucking good, angel. My perfect little whore," he grunts, pinching my nipples, his lips on my neck.

"Fuck, Dorian," I cry, my arms flying behind my head to wrap around his neck. He sinks his teeth into my shoulder until I feel the skin break, pain flaring alongside indescribable pleasure. Bastian watches us with a hooded gaze, letting go of one of my legs to pinch my clit.

"Yes," I hiss, twisting my hands in Dorian's hair, pulling as hard as I can. "Make me come, big brothers. Fuck me. Make me yours. Fill me up. Show me how much I belong to you."

Dorian releases my shoulder from his teeth, small droplets of blood left behind on his lip. He yanks my head back, my scalp burning as his eyes flash with a beast-like hunger, the control he holds so dear gone. Excitement sparkles in my veins, tingles running all over my skin.

"You are mine, little sister. I don't need to make you mine. You've always been so," he snarls, pumping his hips faster.

"Prove it," I say, tempting the monster. A dangerous game to play, but I cannot deny the thrill it gives me.

Bastian chuckles slowly, moving his thumb over my clit at a leisurely place. Dorian's smirk widens, a feral gleam in his eyes. He tuts, shaking his head, but I feel his cock jump inside of me and a stutter in his movements. "My dark little angel. You're going to regret that."

He slips out of me, pushing on my back, making Bastian walk backwards until he falls onto the bed. Bas keeps his hands on my thighs, shuffling backwards until he's laid flat, his interlocked hands resting behind his head. He smiles, giving me a wink, and I grin back.

I try to sit up, but Dorian is already there, pushing me back down. My cheek rests on Bastian's chest, his heart beating rapidly under my ear. A cock pushes against my sex, and I sink down onto it, loving the fullness it gives me. Bastian grunts, moaning, his hands flying to my hips to still my movements. I frown, wiggling on the cock, feeling more stretched than I did before. Bastian moans again, his eyelashes fluttering as he bites his bottom lip. I realise that it's him inside me, not Dorian.

"Rian?" I twist my head to check he's okay, that I didn't push it too far, but he fists my hair and keeps me still.

"Don't move," he orders, and both Bas and I go still. I check Bastian's face, making sure everything's okay, but he gives nothing away.

Warm liquid trails down my ass cheeks, making me jolt and squeal. A loud crack hits the air, and a searing pain forms on my left check, making my eyes sting.

"I said keep still," Dorian barks.

I whimper, resting my head on Bastian's chest again, letting the glorious glow of pain trickle through me. More liquid runs down my ass, and Dorian spreads it, fingers skimming around my hole. Bastian sucks in a breath and mutters a curse that has me curious what Dorian is doing to him.

I don't get a chance to ask as Dorian's fingers slowly fill my ass, twisting and turning, stretching me out. "Relax, angel," he says softly. "Do you trust me?"

There isn't a pause in my answer. "With everything that I have."

He pauses in his movements, placing a kiss on my spine. "That is a gift I do not deserve but one I will treasure, angel."

Tears fill my eyes, and I arch my back into his kiss on my spine, his fingers sinking deeper. He pauses there for a few seconds before stretching me again, adding another finger, making my breath stutter.

"That's my good girl. You are both behaving so well for me." He takes his fingers away, lining his cock up, and my body quivers. "You both belong to me. You are both mine, and I will protect you always."

He pushes his cock inside, adding more warm liquid as he goes. I cry out on Bastian's chest, feeling fuller than I ever have before.

"Holy fucking shit," Bastian hisses. "I can feel you, Dorian. I can fucking feel your cock sliding against mine."

I clench on both their cocks, make us all groan. The fact that they can feel each other makes it so much hotter.

"Looks like little sister likes that you can feel my cock, little brother," Dorian says darkly. He pulls out only to sink back in, making Bastian and I cry out in pleasure. Dorian grabs my hair, lifting me up to whisper in my ear. "Would you like to me to fuck his ass while you watch?"

"Yes," I say immediately as Bastian shouts, "No!"

I chuckle at his wide-eyed protest, making them groan again. "If she wants to watch one of us getting ass fucked, it will be my cock in yours, *Rian.*"

I don't see what Dorian does, but Bastian scowls, shaking his head. He jolts forward, gripping Dorian around the throat, pulling us all down and onto him. He keeps his throat hold, jolting his hips, topping from the bottom as he fucks me. I twist my head to see Dorian turning red, but he doesn't stop Bas.

"Kiss your big brother, Octavia, as he fights desperately to breathe."

Bas forces our faces together, and Dorian's tongue immediately searches mine out, not caring that he cannot breathe. He makes a choked groan, pulling his hips back, fucking me in the ass, both of them working together so there is not a moment I'm empty.

Dorian is the one being choked, but it's me who feels like she's going to pass out from lack of oxygen. Pleasure builds in my stomach, heat rolling down my spine, toes curling. I grab on to them both like I'm going to lose them, trying to fuse us together so we can never be torn apart. Dorian sucks in a deep breath, coughing and choking a little on my lips, but he doesn't stop our kiss.

"Come for us one more time, little sister. Come on your brother's cock," Bas moans. He rolls his hips so my clit grinds on him, and Dorian digs his fingers into my sides, the bite of pain exactly what I need.

My orgasm rolls through me so hard, I see stars. I scream their names, my throat hoarse, my eyes rolling to the back of my head. They grunt in pleasure, my legs shaking as the orgasm hits. They both moan my name, their releases spilling inside me as they kiss my neck, breasts, lips. Bastian's declaration of love again is the last thing I hear before everything goes black.

15

OCTAVIA

Bastian's warm breath hits me in the face, and my eyes crack open, watching him sleep. A smile tugs at my lips, a joyful peace settling in my bones. I reach my fingers to his forehead, brushing his hair out of his eyes. His nose twitches like a bunny, making me giggle, but it's followed by a god-awful noise that has my face screwing up. Bas sleeps like the dead and snores like a damn warthog. I've forgotten that since I've been away.

"Bas," I whisper, shaking him, pushing his side to roll him over. He snorts once more, hiccupping a weird noise before he moves, hugging the covers to his chest.

I roll my eyes, stretching out in bed, groaning at all my aches and pains, the worst being my ass. It stings like a motherfucker, especially on my left check where Dorian spanked me last. He must have hit me harder than I thought and the pleasure I was feeling at the time dulled it, because it's stinging like a bitch now.

We're in their bed; I can tell from the scent of the sheets—it's not in the sex room they had me in last night. Shit, I actually fucked my brothers last night... at the same time...for hours after seeing that they tortured our father for me.

I squeal like a schoolgirl, kicking my legs in the sheets, rolling to the other side to search for Dorian, but I find it empty. Jolting up, I scan the room, but he's nowhere in sight. Jumping out of bed, not worrying if I wake Bas, I search but come up empty. A sense of worry pools in my stomach, my hands becoming sweaty, heart beating out of rhythm. I gnaw my lip, hugging my waist, trying to calm the feeling.

There's never been a time where I've fallen asleep in their bed and they both haven't been there when I've woken. It's strange I've never noticed that before, but his absence has sent a tremble of foreboding down my spine.

After using the bathroom and cleaning up somewhat, I leave a snoring Bastian in bed and go in search of Rian, wearing only an oversized white t-shirt. It smells like Bas, and I hum a little at the reminder.

The staff nod their heads at me as I pass some of them by, some of them giving me a double look, while others give a knowing gaze. I flush at the ones who purse their lips or raise an eyebrow, but none of them say anything to me—they wouldn't dare.

I don't find Dorian in the lounge, the dining room, or the kitchen. I shocked the cooks as I came barrelling in, but they quickly turned it into a warm welcome and insisted I not leave without a bowl full of strawberries. They wanted to make me some pancakes as well to go with them, but something inside me is pulling me towards finding Rian. The longer it takes to find him, the worse it gets.

"You sure he left a message to say he was arriving tomorrow?"

I hear his voice echoing in the halls and rush towards it.

"Yes. He asked for his usual room to be made up, but..."

I turn the corner and skid behind it again, poking my head out. Dorian is speaking to Ghost, Father's head of security... Well, I guess he works for Dorian and Bastian now... Maybe... I don't know what is going on, honestly. All I know is that man still scares the living crap out of me.

Ghost is a nickname given to him by the bloodline. I doubt anyone knows his real one. He got it because he acts like an actual ghost; you don't know he's there unless he wants you to. The hunter of secrets, the invisible killer, the monster in the shadows—if you are his target, there is no hope for you.

There have been plenty of times he was the one who caught me when I was sneaking around as a child, appearing out of nowhere to drag me to my punishment. He forced me to witness the mutilated bodies he had worked on, locked me in a room while he carved up a fresh one, still alive... still screaming. Sometimes, it would be hours, while others, a few minutes, but each time came with a warning.

"This is what happens to people who do not do what they're told, little mouse. This is what will become of you if you continue to not fucking listen. Do you want to die? Do you want to be the next one they send me after?"

Each time, it was the same threat, but he never once told my father he caught me snooping. My brothers would be the only one he told, every time without fail. Dorian would tell me off until I cried, and then Bastian would take me to the cooks for ice-cream.

"Spit it out, Ghost. I would like to get back to bed. I have more pressing things to do," Dorian snaps, checking the time on his pocket watch.

Ghost's face screws up in disgust, but his expression drops before Dorian can catch it. He rubs a tattooed hand across the back of his neck, a flash of fear in his gaze. "He's asked for another room to be set up for a guest."

Dorian snaps the watch closed, his head shooting up as he frowns hard. "A *guest?* Are you sure?"

"Very," he says, nodding once. "I believe it could be what we... *you* feared."

What he feared? What did Dorian fear?

"Very well," Dorian muses, tilting his head side to side, his calculating eyes flickering back and forth, working on an idea. I see it the moment it happens: the tiny worry on his face disappears, and a cunning, cruel smirk tugs at his lips instead. "Set up the room, but make sure the guest is in the west wing."

Ghost matches his smirk, raising an eyebrow, which Rian matches. He chuckles hauntingly in that weird way of his, sending me back to my childhood. Ghost's laugh always scared me. He's a hauntingly beautiful man, but in a run for your life type of way.

"I believe I know the perfect room to set the guest up in. Congratulations, by the way. I forgot to say it earlier," he says, slapping Dorian on the shoulder and walking away. "Welcome home, little mouse. It's good to have you back."

He flicks me a look over his shoulder, and I scowl back at him. I hate that nickname; he always called me a mouse finding herself in places she shouldn't be. Of course, the ghost knew I was here watching, and from the unsurprised look on Dorian's face, so did he.

He crosses his arms over his chest, frowning hard at me as I step out from behind the corner.

"Morning, big brother," I say, smiling innocently. "Strawberry?" I hold out the bowl, making my smile bigger, batting my eyelashes.

"I distinctly remember telling you that you're not allowed to walk through this manor without Bastian or I at your side." He strolls towards me, his frown deepening with each step. Placing a finger under my chin, he lifts my head, leaning down. "That is twice now you have broken our rule. Are you having problems with your memory, little sister?"

My fingers search the bowl in my hands for a strawberry without breaking his imploring gaze, bringing one to my lips and taking a bite.

The sweetness makes my taste buds sing, juice dripping down the corner of my mouth onto my chin. Dorian tries to resist watching, but his eyes keep flickering as he gulps hard, his grip on my chin tightening.

"My memory works just fine, big brother," I husk. "I just don't enjoy following the rules. I will never follow rules again. Shattering every rule got me you."

"I will punish you every time you break a rule, Octavia," he mutters, pushing me against the wall. His free hand grips my thigh, pressing himself tight against me.

"Good. I like your punishments." I drag the half bitten strawberry across his lips, painting them pink. He opens his mouth and takes the whole thing, biting my fingers, his tongue lapping up the juices. "How would you like to punish me?"

His eyes go hooded, his nostrils flaring as he lifts me from my feet, wrapping my legs around him. The bowl of strawberries shatters to the floor, and he unzips himself faster than I can blink, lining himself up.

"Already wet and ready for me, angel?"

He runs the head of his cock through my slit, and I moan, my head hitting the wall. "Always."

There's never a time I'm not ready for him. I will never tire of him, will never be bored or unhappy. He has always been my protector, and I will always be his safe haven. No one can understand what we have gone through, the life we have lived, our future.

"I love you, Dorian. I have loved you my entire life in different ways, but there has never been one second where I didn't. I have always been yours," I whisper, unable to hold back my feelings, saying them out loud for anyone to hear.

Dorian freezes, his eyes wide, mouth opening and closing before his jaw clenches. Tears fill my eyes, but I understand it, understand *him*, more than anyone could.

"It's okay," I whisper, leaning my forehead against his. "You don't need to say it. You've shown me how you feel for years. I don't need the words. I just need you, Dorian. Only you."

Out of the three of us, Dorian had the hardest time, raised to be Father's successor. He's the one who has always struggled with feelings and showing any type of emotion. I meant what I said: I don't need to hear him say it to know he loves me.

"Angel," he whispers, but he's cut off with the clattering of dishes and a squeal of surprise.

"Oh... oh my... I didn't mean..." A maid flutters on the floor, frozen to the spot, staring at us.

We stare at her, as frozen as she is. My heart beats wildly, but I cannot deny the wetness pooling on the tip of Dorian's cock, the excitement of being caught sending me wild.

"Fuck me, big brother," I order, pushing down on him.

He whirls his head, a pleasantly surprised smile on his face. "Well, if my little sister wants to be fucked, who am I to deny her?"

He forces his way inside, filling me up, making my body ache and burn with the soreness of last night. I chase the pain and pleasure, rolling my hips, wrapping my hands around his neck.

"I'm so sorry, sir. I will leave you to it. I didn't mean-"

We ignore the maid, lost in each other. Every roll of my hips, my clit hits his stomach, and he grabs my hips, tilting just right so the head of his cock hits that sweet spot inside me. I cry out at the angle, working faster to chase the blaze of bliss he fills me with.

"I love you, Dorian," I cry as he sinks inside me. "I love you so much, and I will tell you that every day until you realise you are worthy of it. I will tell you until my throat bleeds, until you realise you deserve it."

His hips stutter, and he takes in a deep breath, fury on his face. From my words or because I know his secret, I'm not sure. He doesn't believe he is worthy of love. I've seen it all my life; he does everything for me and Bastian. He constantly makes sure we are both okay, but he always holds himself back, watching us have fun but never joining in.

His hands wrap around my throat, cutting off my oxygen, his nostrils flaring as he squeezes. His hips pounds faster, fucking me against the wall as I hold on tight. I mouth the words I love you again, not stopping even as he chokes me. He releases my throat, crashing his lips to mine, and I suck in a lungful of air, breathing him in.

"Octavia," he moans, fucking me harder and faster. "I'm supposed to be the one poisoning you, twisting your heart until it only beats for us, not the other way around. You have no idea what you do to me."

I move my body against his, taking him as deep as I can, pleasure swirling in my stomach with every brush of my clit against him. His cock pulses inside me, and I tighten around him on each one, making him grunt. Reaching for his tie, I move it off his collar onto his neck, and pull the end until the knot tightens, cutting off his oxygen, choking *him*.

His eyes blaze, and his movements become feral. His fingers cut into the top of my thighs so hard, I wouldn't be surprised if he drew blood. My head slams against the wall, and I can no longer move but enjoy the ride, holding onto his tie for dear life as his face turns red.

"You did poison me, Dorian. You infected me with your darkness, but you forgot that you're not immune yourself."

I tug his tie harder, pushing my back against the wall, jolting forward to make him fall. We tumble to the ground, but he keeps his hands on my thighs, not attempting to break his fall, and lands with a loud bang. His cock—impressively—stays inside me, throbbing harder than ever. He tries to lift himself up and take control, but I push on his chest, forcing him to stay down, tugging the tie with the other.

"My turn now, big brother." I roll my hips with each word, enjoying his muted grunts of pleasure. "While you were busy trying to pull me to the dark side, you didn't realise I was shining the light on you. You love me, Dorian Stone. I know you love me; I don't need the words from you. You think you tricked me into loving you, but I'm the one who let it happen."

I lean forward, continuing to slowly grind on him, high on the pleasure, placing my lips on his. "Come for me, big brother, the one you are totally and completely in love with."

He lets out a silent moan, bruising my thighs in his grip, his hips stuttering underneath me. My orgasm explodes at the same time, and I cry my relief into his mouth. He lets go of my leg, searching for something, and produces a gleaming knife, cutting the tie strangling him. He gasps for breath, gulping in lungfuls of air before fisting my hair and bringing me in for a scorching kiss.

"You can be such a brat, Octavia," he grunts breathlessly. "Almost bloody killed me then."

I giggle against his lips, pulling back, unable to hold my smile in. "Lucky you love me then, isn't it?"

He scowls, slapping my ass, sending a searing pain across it that has me screaming.

"What the hell?"

That slap shouldn't have hurt as much as it did—it wasn't that hard. I twist my head around, but I can't see anything at this angle. I turn back to Dorian, his scowl gone, replaced by a smirk.

"What have you done?"

I know that smirk, and I especially know that excited glee on his face. It's the one he always gives when he gets one up on something with Bastian. I don't like this.

"Come on, angel, it's time to wake our brother up. I believe he was saying last night how he wanted to eat that sweet pussy of yours after I filled you up."

He moves us quickly, standing up and chucking me over his shoulder. I squeal at the motion, slapping his ass, kicking my legs. "What have you done, Rian?"

Teeth sink into my ass cheek, the one causing me pain, and I scream, trying to wriggle away, but he holds me tight. He chuckles against my skin, dragging his tongue across where he just took a bite, soothing it. What the fuck has he done?

16

BASTIAN

I'm enjoying my fantastic pancake breakfast, humming a happy little tune to myself, licking the syrup from my fingers, tasting sweet goodness along with sickly syrup. Nothing tastes better than Octavia's sweet pussy. I made sure not to wash my hands before we came down for breakfast, wanting to keep her on me for as long as possible.

Never thought waking up unable to breathe, fighting for my life, would be on my list of things I never want to live without, but having it be because Octavia was sitting on top of me, her pussy on my lips begging for my touch? Well, that changes everything. She didn't sit there willingly; it was more like she was forced. Dorian tied her up with his tie and held her there while she alternated between moaning in pleasure at my tongue and threatening to cut his balls off. Both things were an enormous turn on.

Now I'm the only one enjoying their breakfast. Pretty girl didn't like the present Dorian gave her last night when she was passed out between us, and Dorian doesn't like that she is now giving him the silent treatment.

"Sooo," I say, prolonging the word. "How is everyone doing this beautiful morning?"

Octavia scowls across the table, stabbing her sausage and aggressively cutting it, beautiful bite marks and bruises decorating her skin.

She refused to sit next to us, plopping herself down in her usual seat. I tried to sit next to her, but she almost stabbed me in the dick. I love her, but that is a bit too kinky, even for me. Dorian has a matching scowl directed at me, and I shrug my shoulders, going back to licking my fingers.

"How long do you believe this little tantrum is going to last? We have things to discuss. Things that require you to participate in the conversation," Dorian says, taking a sip of his tea.

Octavia's cutlery clatters to the side, and pure, unhinged anger filters into her gaze that has my dick hardening. I grip it tight, adjusting myself in my jeans. I'm pretty sure this would be a bad time to suggest she crawl on her hands and knees and choke on my dick while I finish eating, but then again, maybe...

"Tantrum? *Tantrum*?" she spits. "You tattooed your names on my ass when I was passed out! I am not having a *little fucking tantrum*. I'm trying really hard not to murder you both!"

Okay, so maybe it's not the right time.

"Hey, I didn't do the tattooing," I exclaim. It may have been my suggestion, but I wasn't the actual transgressor.

"Please," she hisses. "This idea has your name written all over it."

"Literally." Dorian smirks.

And that breaks the tiny thread holding her sanity. She flies across the table, knocking over everything in her way, a knife in each hand. She wildly stabs at us, going for the more fatal spots.

Damn, pretty girl is super pissed.

I grab her fast, before she can inflict major damage, letting her nick Dorian on the arm first and sticking my tongue out as he huffs. She thrashes against my chest, screaming in frustration as I wrap her in a bear hug.

"If you keep wiggling like that, I'll have no choice but bend you over and take you right here on the table. Maybe I'll get Dorian to add some more ink to your pretty ass. I do like my name there."

She hisses like a feral cat, baring her teeth at me. "Don't you dare."

"Then stop wiggling and I won't." She forces herself to calm down or at least remain still, but I can't help winding her up again. "At least I won't for now. No promises as soon as we leave this room. I'm thinking of a skull next," I whisper in her ear.

"Son of a cunt," she yells, thrashing once more. "You will not tattoo my body without my consent."

I laugh hysterically, keeping her in a bear hug on my lap as she tries to stab me again. Blonde hair flies everywhere, her cute pink skirt riding up her thighs, showing purple finger-shaped bruises on them. I wonder if she's as turned on as I am. I cup her pussy, feeling her soaking wet panties, and groan, grinding my dick against her ass. I fucking knew it.

"Motherfucker," I hiss, pulling my hand away. Sneaky little angel sliced my forearm in my distraction. She grins at me wide with all teeth, bloodthirsty rage gleaming in her eyes.

I am so fucking horny.

"I was thinking a winter wedding sounded ideal. Only a couple months away, plenty of time to plan. What do you think, angel?" Dorian interrupts, throwing the question out calmly, cutting into his poached egg and taking a bite.

I'm pretty sure there's a whole ritual that is supposed to be done with this, and what he did is not it. But it's sure going to be interesting.

Octavia goes dead still on my lap, the fight leaving her instantly. Her face scrunches up, nose wrinkling in that adorable way it does when she's confused, and I bop her nose, unable to help myself. She slaps my hand away, scrunching her face hard with a scowl.

"Does that not work for you?" Dorian asks.

She shakes her head, relaxed now in my hold. "I'm sorry, have I missed something? Who's getting married, and why are we talking about this right now?"

Oh, what a cute, innocent little angel.

Dorian places his cutlery down, grabbing a napkin and wiping his mouth delicately—fancy bastard. "We are, of course. Please pay attention, Octavia."

She splutters, jolting forward, her mouth hanging open.

"You haven't even asked me!" she exclaims, her eyes widening, jumping out of my arms and I let her, standing between us. "How am I supposed to know you were talking about us? I've only just got back. We've only just started this thing between us, and you're talking about a wedding...marriage? How...what?"

Her breathing gets faster and faster as she paces in the little space between us, pulling at her hair. Dorian and I eye each other, coming to the same conclusion. We pushed her too far, and I think we might have actually broken her. Perfect.

I jump to my feet the same time Dorian does, me at her back and him at her front, caging her in, consuming her. "Breathe, pretty girl. We got you," I whisper in her ear, holding her flush against me.

Dorian grasps her chin, forcing her to stare into his eyes. We've got this move down to a science. She used to have panic attacks a lot when she was younger, and the only thing that helped was Dorian making her focus on him while I trapped her in my grasp, giving her entire body comfort, security.

"It doesn't matter that you've only just gotten home. This right here hasn't just started. There's not been one moment in your life when you weren't ours. When we weren't yours," Dorian husks, a surprising amount of emotion in his tone. "The second you came on our cocks, your fate was sealed. There's no escaping us, Octavia. You are our universe, and we are your ride to hell."

I graze my lips along the shell of her ear, flicking my tongue, enjoying her shiver. "We've killed for you. We would die for you. We can't step into the light with you, but we can drag you into the darkness. We are the demons of your nightmares, and we're never letting you go."

Dorian scowls at that little sprinkle of truth I slipped in there. She'll think it's a metaphor, and that's fine. Boring bastard made me promise not to say anything about the nightmares until it's the right time, worried she won't be able to handle it. I think she'll find it hilarious, or maybe she'll try to slit our throats. Either way, it's a win in my book; I'll be balls deep inside her afterwards.

"I'll ask again: is winter a good time for our wedding?" Dorian asks, pressing his lips against hers.

She gulps hard, her body quivering as she wipes her palms on her skirt. Her head tilts to gaze up at me, a stunned, questioning glint in her eyes. I wink, ducking down for a kiss, biting her bottom lip and releasing it with a pop. Her lashes flutter as she turns back to Dorian.

"I... We..." She shakes her head, blinking rapidly, and like a flip of a switch, her body relaxes, sinking into us. "I'd prefer autumn, I suppose."

Dorian gives a quick nod, a satisfied smirk on his face, while I try not to squeeze her to death in excitement. I pick her up and spin her around, her joyful giggle tinkling through the room, bouncing off the walls, making my heart stutter.

"Autumn it is," Dorian says, a tiny smile on his face at the two of us. "Now get over here and sit on my lap so we can tattoo a ring on you."

Octavia's giggle cuts off mid laugh, her face dropping as the fury she had a few minutes ago comes rushing back.

"Tattoo?!"

Uh-oh. Should not have said that. I would not like to be the one on the end of that tone.

"If you think we would put a ring on your finger that could easily come off, then you still have some things to learn, little si-"

Oh shit!

Octavia rears her arm back and clocks Dorian in the throat, cutting him off mid-word. He splutters, grabbing his neck, wheezing, almost doubled over. I cackle with laughter, holding my stomach as I wipe tears from my eyes.

"Pretty girl, that was awesom-"

Fuck!

She knees me right in the balls, and I fall to the floor like a sack of shit. Should have seen that coming. She glares at us, marching out of the room with her middle finger in the air, slamming the door behind her.

Dorian and I stare at each other, trying to get our breath back, then laugh gleefully like the carefree kids we never got to be.

I fucking love that woman.

17

OCTAVIA

"Stupid." *Swing.*

"Controlling." *Swing.*

"Bull headed." *Swing.*

"Manic, psychotic, bastards!"

I scream each word, swinging my bat, destroying everything in their room. Bastian's hiding spot for all his favourite weapons is still the same place, and the wooden bat covered in barbed wire screamed my name, tempting me to pick it up and permanently damage something that belonged to them like they did to me.

Nothing in my life has been in my control. Not my clothes, my hair, my make-up, what I eat. *Nothing.* I try to take control of my body in any way I can with what little means I have. They took that away just a little more with something permanent—another thing someone controlled.

"Fuck you," I screech, swinging my bat against a huge wooden chest, hitting it repeatedly until my joints burned. Black feathers fall out of the cracks I'm making, floating in the air around me.

"What the…" I mutter, a feather flying into my face, tickling my nose. The feeling of déjà vu swamps my veins, the image extremely familiar.

"Wow. Now this is what I call a tantrum. What the fuck did they do, little mouse?"

Ghost's deep voice makes me jump, the hairs on the back of my neck standing on end. He's right behind me, silently entering the room, his footsteps so quiet that I didn't even realise it.

"I am *not* having a tantrum," I seethe, taking a few steps back. Dorian would scold me for that move. *'Never show them any weakness, even when you're so terrified, you think your heart is about to stop.'*

I've never been fantastic at that. I was born wrong in more ways than one when it comes to this family. Prey in a family of predators, they always used to say, but they used to promise that they would be my demons in a world of monsters.

My demons. Huh.

"You really don't call this a tantrum?" Ghost extends his arms, swooping around at the mess I caused.

Clothes are scattered everywhere on the floor, the wardrobes and drawers splintered and shattered. Their mirrors are smashed, Dorian's chair has chunks taken out of it where the barbed wire caught it. The mattress on the bed is destroyed.

It's not like I *hate* their names on my body. In fact, when I think about it, a warm glow seeps through my stomach at being branded, being owned by them. But it should have been *my* choice. Still, I might have gone a bit overboard on destroying all their stuff, especially the two things I left on the tattered bed.

I took Bastian's favourite knife and hammered it until it was bent into a weird shape, rendering it unusable. Before I destroyed the knife, I used it to stab and rip the pages of Dorian's favourite book: a signed first edition of Dracula by Bram Stoker.

Shit, I took it too far.

"Someone's looking nervous. Poor little mouse scared?" Ghost taunts as I bite my bottom lip, staring at the unsalvageable items.

"Shut up," I snap, pointing the bat at him. "And stop calling me a mouse. I'm not a child for you to torment."

He tilts his head to the side, examining me. It's not in a creepy, pervy way; he's not checking me out, more like sizing me up.

"You're right, you're not a child anymore." He takes a few steps forward, placing a hand on my shoulder. I hold the bat under his chin, pushing it up, but he stays unbothered, maybe a bit amused.

"You're not the scared little mouse you were as a child, but do you think you have what it takes to survive in this bloodline? To survive *them*?" He purses his lips, shaking his head. "I'm not sure."

He lets me go with a jolt, and I feel like I've been punched in the gut because I don't know the answer to his question. I don't know if I can survive it all, but I do know I will die trying if it means I get to have them, no matter for how short a time.

Ghost grabs the chest I was smashing on the floor, still just about in one piece, and eyes it with disdain, grunting as he picks it up. As he gets to the door, he turns, giving me a look I can't quite figure out.

"I didn't do or show you those things when you were younger to torment you." He blows a strand of platinum blond hair out of his eyes, the small wrinkles around them deepening.

"Then why did you?" I ask, frowning. I always assumed he did it because he was a deranged bastard like everyone else.

He sighs heavily, looking me up and down, but again, not in a creepy way. "I was trying to make sure you made it into adulthood within the bloodline. To make sure you *survived*, Octavia."

He pauses for a second, and it looks like he's about to say something else, but two throats clear loudly, interrupting us. He twists to find Bastian and Dorian glaring at him. Bas has his arms crossed, clenching his hands, while Rian raises an eyebrow, a challenging gaze in his eyes.

Ghost turns around once more to me, a small smile on his face. I don't think I've ever seen him smile. "Luckily I wasn't the only one trying."

He bows his head to me once and walks past my brothers, leaving me more confused than ever.

"What was that about?" I mutter, unsure if I'm asking them or myself. The question doesn't matter, though, as they don't answer me.

Dorian and Bastian slowly walk into the room, their shoes crunching on broken glass, kicking bits of wood and clothing out of their path, their attention on the items I left on the bed.

"I didn't mean to," I say straight away, taking a step closer but halting as they pick up their items.

Bastian gasps audibly, clutching the knife to his chest, rocking and soothing it like a baby. "Aww, my poor girl. What happened to you?"

"Bas-"

"It looks like this was done intentionally, angel. Pray tell, how did you *accidentally* do this?" Dorian places the book down gently on the bed before twisting towards me, pursing his lips, waiting for an answer.

I shuffle from side to side, the barbed wire bat still clutched in my hand. I can't let go of it.

"I... I was angry. I wasn't thinking straight, I wanted to hurt you as much as you hurt me," I confess softly, feeling childish in my tit for tat.

"She will never be the same," Bastian cries dramatically. "Ruined. My poor baby ruined, and I wasn't here to watch her last moments. Oh, sweet, dark mother, I'm begging you to bring her back to life. Take away my grief."

He twirls, falling gracefully onto the bed, the back of his hand on his forehead, still clutching the knife to his chest, only laying there for about a second before sitting back up, sending me a wink. Half my worry and fear disappears at his playfulness, and I let out a small giggle, unable to hold it in. Bas is never mad at me, no matter what I do. Dorian, on the other hand...

"You wanted to hurt us as much as we hurt you?" He phrases it as a question, but he doesn't expect me to answer. "How have we hurt you, Octavia? By protecting you all your life? By being your constant, your lifeline, by making us yours as much as you are ours?"

The rage from earlier trickles in, and the more he talks, the more red I see. My grip on the bat tightens, my fingers flexing around the handle.

"By taking away a choice about my body. *My* body, Dorian, not yours," I say, slicing the bat through the air. "That tattoo should have been my choice, as well as having a ring tattooed on my finger. You don't get to decide that for me. Everything in my goddamn life has always been decided, but my body is *mine*."

Dorian's face morphs into a smile so fast, it has my emotions pausing. "That's my girl." He smirks, Bastian joining him with a matching grin.

"What?"

They take a step towards me, but I hold up the bat, keeping distance between us. My mind is doing somersaults.

"Easy, pretty girl. We wanted you to react this way. I didn't think you would go for our second most prized possessions, but we wanted you to lose your shit on us."

"Again, *what*?" I shout, swinging the bat as they take another step.

"It was a test, I suppose you can say, as well as a punishment for breaking the rules. I needed to see you'd push back," Dorian says, pushing up against the bat, the top resting on his chest. "You're ours, little sister. We want to consume you, fucking devour you, but we don't want to you to get lost in us."

"We want you to get lost *with* us," Bastian says. "Follow us down the path to hell, pretty girl."

Okay. *Okay*. I can kind of see where they were coming from, but-

"Was there seriously no other way to take this little test without you putting your names on my ass like some fucking stamp?"

Fucking men!

Their heads swivel to gaze at each other as they shrug their shoulders and speak in sync. "No."

"Of course not." I sigh, lowering the bat.

As soon as I drop it, they slot into their spots, Bas holding me tight, letting me feel his hardness against my ass. "That was so fucking hot, seeing you with my bat. I want to watch you bash someone's head in with it, covering yourself in blood, and then I'll fuck you over their still-warm corpse."

I shiver, partly in disgust and partly totally turned on. *So fucked up.*

Dorian takes the bat from my hand, peeling my fingers off it, dropping it to the floor. He brings my hand to his lips, kissing my ring finger with a look in his eyes that has my heart racing.

"We're clear on the *no tattooing Octavia's finger until she agrees*, right?" I say, a flutter of panic rising in my chest. Bastian's arms slowly wrap further around my waist, and I try to take my hand from Dorian's grasp, but he doesn't let go.

"*Right?*"

Dorian laughs deeply, shaking his head, a haunting, feral gleam in his eyes. "I don't think we agreed to that, did we, brother?"

Bastian laughs manically, lifting my feet from the ground in another bear hug. "Nah, I don't remember agreeing to that. Especially not after

she destroyed the two things that are almost as precious to us as she is."

Wait, I'm the most precious thing to them? They said the things I destroyed were the second most, both of which I got as birthday gifts for their eighteenth.

"Tie her to the bed, Bastian. Time for our wife to wear our ring."

Wife?

Bastian carries me towards the bed, and Dorian pulls red ropes from inside his jacket. It snaps me to life, and I thrash in his grip.

"Son's of bitches. You bastards, I haven't said yes yet!"

"Exactly, pretty girl. You just said yet, so that means you're going to at some point. We're just jumping ahead a few chapters," Bastian says before he nips my shoulder.

"Motherfuckers, that's not the point."

Bas throws me onto the bed, laying on top of me as I try to sit up and flee. He spreads my limbs like a goddamn starfish, all the while grinning in my face as Dorian ties me up.

I'm so going to get them for this.

18

DORIAN

"I'm going to kill you. Both of you. You are so freaking dea-"

She keeps trying to threaten us between gasps of pleasure and hisses of pain. *Adorable*.

Bastian is between her spread legs, flicking his tongue over her swollen clit, lapping up her release and burying his face deeper, inhaling her scent as I finish the tattoo on her ring finger. I could have given her a simple band, which would have been much quicker, but our wife deserves better.

"If you keep wiggling, this will take much longer. How many times has Bastian made you come now: three, four? Your sweet cunt must be desperate for relief."

Her head twists to me, blonde hair stuck to her face. She glares hard, fire in her gaze as she tries to hold it, but Bastian does something that has her whimpering, biting her swollen bottom lip and shaking. I smirk, pulling her bottom lip from her teeth and biting it myself. She keens as she kisses me deeper, her tongue seeking mine out. I release her lip and give her what she wants, caught off guard when her sensual kiss turns to pain. It's my turn to hiss as she sucks my tongue into her mouth, biting down on it fiercely until I taste copper.

I fist her hair, pulling her closer to me instead of away, taking all the pain she can give, my breathing ragged. I'm fucking obsessed with the pain she gives me. Little sister has another thing coming if she thinks that would make me pull away. My cock is harder than ever.

She pulls back on a gasp, my blood tinting her lips. "Sick bastard," she gasps.

"Twisted bitch." I smirk.

Her eyes widen for a second before they go hooded, and she smirks back sensually. "True."

Her lashes flutter, eyes rolling to the back of her head as she keens, arching her back, legs shaking against the binds. Bastian groans, grinding his hips into the bed, probably aching for relief as she squirts all over his face. He keeps going until she screams, telling him to stop, tears welling in her eyes.

He lifts his head, gasping for breath, covered in her cum. I fist his shirt, pulling him up her body before running my tongue over his chin and lips, tasting her off him. He willingly lets me, poking out his tongue in a challenge, his eyes on her. I hear her whine, feeling the movement of her legs as she tries to create some friction, clearly turned on from her big brothers playing together. I suck his tongue into my mouth, catching every drop of her left.

"Just hurry and finish the tattoo before I spontaneously combust," she snaps.

Releasing Bastian, I chuckle as she throws her head back onto the pillow, moaning in frustration. I slip into the chair beside the bed, grabbing her bound hand and picking up the tattoo gun. I perfected tattooing when I was a teenager and Bastian wanted to get his first one. He started getting tattoos for me.

I've always had an obsession with my siblings—the need to protect them, to be there for them, for them to be mine and no one else's. I wanted to brand them so everyone knew they were not to be touched, so they knew they could never belong to anyone else. On a drunken night in our teens, I let it slip to Bastian what I wanted to do, but it wasn't with tattoos. No, it was carving them up and scarring them in beautiful patterns as their blood spilled.

The next day, Bastian told me it would be a bit too much for our little sister, but he didn't make me feel like I was crazy. Instead, he gave me the idea of tattoos and told me his body was mine to do with as I pleased. I practised first on dead bodies so I didn't mess it up, and when I gave Bastian his first tattoo, it calmed some strange part of me and developed a new obsession. Octavia doesn't know how lucky she is that she's only just getting her first ones now.

"There, all done," I say, adding just two more dots that I'd been waiting to finish two orgasms ago.

"That was it? You couldn't have done that half an hour ago?" Octavia says indignantly, cracking open an eye.

I chuckle as I stand, unzipping my trousers, and Bastian does the same. "I could have, but then I wouldn't have been able to watch your body shake uncontrollably or hear all the ways you plan to kill us."

Bastian laughs wildly as she swears, gripping his shaft tight as he kneels between her legs. I place my hand in front of her mouth as I order, "spit."

She licks her lips, eyeing my hand. "Slowly," she mutters.

"Slowly what, pretty girl?" Bastian asks, jerking his cock faster.

She flicks her gaze back and forth between us, her doe eyes becoming more like sirens. "When the time comes, I plan to kill you slowly, making it last weeks, dragging out your deaths until the point your body smells and looks like a corpse while you're still alive."

"Shit," Bastian grunts, fucking his fist, his eyes rolling to the back of his head.

"Spit!" I bark, on the verge of coming without touching myself just at that visual of Octavia drenched in our blood, standing over us manically, unhinged, bloodthirsty for revenge. It's the sexiest thing I can imagine.

She leans forward, spitting onto my hand, and I quickly wrap it around my cock, rubbing my shaft quickly as my balls tighten, lightning shooting down my spine as my orgasm hits me. I grunt out my release, aiming it at her face, and she opens her mouth as she wiggles, catching my cum on her tongue. Bastian curses, his hips stuttering watching us before he paints her cunt with white ropes.

As soon as he finishes, he dives back between her legs, cleaning his cum off with his tongue as Octavia whines, keeping her mouth open and cum-splattered tongue out. She raises an eyebrow, waiting. I wrap my hand around her throat, enjoying her cut off gasp for air. I drag my tongue up her neck, catching the small droplets of cum there, slowly making my way to her mouth before devouring it all, capturing my saltiness and swallowing.

"Good boys," she croaks as I let her go.

Bastian chuckles between her legs, resting his chin on her beautiful soft stomach. "Oh, pretty girl, you are playing with hellfire calling our big brother that."

She smirks evilly, giggling as Bastian tickles her sides. I grasp her chin, and she gives me her best innocent look, trying to stifle her laugh. "It's a good job we have things to do, or I would tattoo my entire face all over your back for that little remark."

Her laugh dies quickly, eyes widening. "You wouldn't?" she stutters, and I raise my eyebrow. "Oh, fuck, you would. It just slipped out—post orgasmic insanity, you could say." She cringes, batting her lashes at me.

"Has he arrived?" Bastian asks, all signs of playfulness gone.

I let go of Octavia's chin, shaking my head. "No, but it will be sooner than he said, I think. We need to get ready."

He gives a curt nod, and we both untie Octavia from the bed. She sits up, rubbing her wrists as Bastian rubs her ankles. As she grasps her left hand, her eyes go wide as she stares at the tattoo.

"It's beautiful," she whispers, tracing the vines and black leaves. I tried to make the leaves as close to a deadly nightshade as I could, which was tricky with them being so small.

I pull her into my arms, kissing her gently. This would be the perfect time to tell her, to say the three words she deserves. "I-"

She looks up at me with those big doe eyes expectantly, hope shining through, and I blow it.

"You're ours, angel. I've wanted to give you this for years. We're never letting you go. As soon as we deal with our grandfather, I want you to brand us as yours."

Her eyes shutter with disappointment, and I hear Bastian huff a breath as he mutters something unintelligible. It's so easy for him. I wish it could be that way for me; they both deserve it.

"Wait," Octavia says, alarmed. "Grandfather is on his way here?"

"Yes." I smirk, pushing the uncomfortable feeling in my gut away. "But first, we have a gift for you. A gift for all of us, really, and it needs to be done before Grandfather gets here."

Bastian takes her from my arms and picks her up, as giddy as can be. We've been waiting our whole lives for this moment.

"Time to visit daddy dearest for the last time ever, pretty girl. Today is his funeral."

19

OCTAVIA

They made me put on one of my best dresses for the occasion and, seeing as it was for our father's funeral, I decided the only appropriate colour would be pink. The dusty pink pleated tulle skirt swishes as I twirl in the mirror, hitting mid-thigh, my hair falling down my back in soft waves. The corset cinches my frame, making my breasts appear fuller. They look fantastic, but my favourite part of the dress is the dainty ribbon shoulder straps that fall down the top of my arms, a bow tying them off. I wanted to wear heels, but Dorian tutted and said they would be too much of a hassle, so I've gone for simple white ballet flats with ribbons that twist and tie up my calves.

Dorian comes up behind me, running his finger across my bare shoulder, staring at me in the mirror. "You look like a ballerina."

"Too much?" I ask, gnawing at my bottom lip.

I've finally got clothes that feel like me—girly, light, and so freaking pretty. No more black or blood red, or outfits approved by my father. But maybe I went too far and cute for Dorian, not sexy enough.

He grasps my chin, twisting me in his grip. "Do you like this outfit?"

"I love this outfit," I admit on a whisper. I was saving this for something special.

"Then that's all that matters. You would look beautiful to me in a rag, Octavia. I want you to be you, not a version you think I want."

He drags his gaze over my body, biting his bottom lip and snaking a hand behind my back, grabbing my ass and pulling me against him. "That being said, I think you look like the most delicious treat in this outfit. The only way it would look better is if it was rucked up around your waist with you bent over and my cock in your ass."

He lets go of my chin, grabbing my ass with both hands and spreading my cheeks, making my face flush. A finger drags over my underwear near my hole, tracing it lightly, making me shiver.

"Would you like that again, angel?" he husks. "Do you want my cock buried deep in your ass while you're begging me to stop because the pleasure is too much?"

His head lowers, resting his lips on mine, and I'm a goner.

"Please."

He chuckles, slowly moving his hands from my ass to my thighs, his fingers pushing past my underwear, dragging up my slit. I whimper against his lips, moving closer, wanting more.

"As soon as you kill our father, I'm going to bend you over his dead body and fuck you until you come, screaming for your big brother."

He grips the back of my hair, plunging two fingers inside me and rubbing my clit with his thumb. I'm so turned on, I'm about to burst. He only goes on for a few seconds, hitting every single pleasure spot I have until I scream, pulling him in for a kiss. It's quick and short before he releases me, not letting me come.

My arousal coats his fingers, and he stares at them, opening his mouth to lick up the mess, but Bastian is quicker. He rushes over, sucking Dorian's fingers into his mouth, humming at the taste of me.

"Better than honey, I fucking swear." Bastian groans, ignoring Dorian's scowl as he grabs a handkerchief from his black suit pocket, wiping Bastian's spit from his fingers.

"Did you have to lick my fingers so much?"

Bastian sends me a wink, smacking his lips together. "To get all of her flavour off you, I most definitely had to lick them like that."

He rushes over to me, grabbing my hand, making me spin in a circle. "Pretty girl, you look absolutely goddamn breathtaking. You're never allowed to wear anything else again." He stops spinning me, pursing his lips. "Although it would be better in white. The blood would have looked fantastic on it if it was white."

I shake my head from the dizziness of his spin—and because Bastian is in a suit. "You're in a suit?" I say, stating the obvious, but he never wears one.

"Thought the occasion called for it. How do I look?"

He holds out his arms and spins in a circle of his own, posing with his hands on his hips at the end. He acts all silly, but I can see the strain in his smile, the twitch of his fingers as he tries not to fuss.

I step into his space, grabbing his black tie and pulling him down. "You look so fucking handsome," I say, and he smiles, but it's a lack-luster one. "I still prefer you in jeans and a t-shirt, though—or nothing at all."

I wink, flicking my tongue out, licking his lips. His grin gets bigger, and he lifts me in the air, forcing my legs around his waist. "You're right. After today, I'll leave the snobby outfits to our snooty big brother. I'll change right after the kill feast."

"I am *not* snooty," Dorian scoffs, raising his nose in the air looking awfully snooty, and I would have laughed if I wasn't for the fact Bastian mentioned a kill feast.

"Is he not dead yet? I thought you killed him?"

At least that was what I assumed while I was getting ready, since they said we were attending his funeral. They never said he was dead, but how else was I supposed to take that?

"He will be," Dorian says, placing a knife in my hand as Bastian places my feet on the ground. "As soon as you run the blade through his heart."

"Or his skull, whichever you prefer. I myself would go for the eyes first," Bastian says.

They move me to face the mirror, standing behind me. Dorian picks something out from his suit pocket before his arms come around my head, placing a black lace masquerade mask over my eyes while Bastian sets a black metal tiara on my head, metal feathers woven through the design.

"Is my dark angel ready to hunt down a monster?" Dorian asks. "We thought about you killing him in your old room, but Bastian convinced me a hunt would be much more fun."

I rear back at him calling me a dark angel. The demons call me a dark angel, and maybe it's time to live up to that name—and who better to start with than our father?

A grin pulls at my lips, and I grip the handle of the knife tight, gazing at Bastian and Dorian in the mirror and finding their matching grins.

"Welcome to fright night, pretty girl. It's gonna be one hell of a game."

20

OCTAVIA

Bastian and Dorian had Ghost unchain Father, pretending to be freeing him. He told him the only way out was through the west dungeons because all the doors and windows were locked, and I'm not sure whether to let him get there.

As I walk through the halls of the castle, I let every bit of anger and hatred course through my veins. I remember each time he beat me, every time he ignored me, all the pain he put us through, sending me away and letting me rot in that awful academy. It builds and builds until I'm shaking with rage with nothing to quench my bloodthirsty need for revenge.

Dorian and Bastian stalk the halls at my side, our footsteps silent. I'm the only one in a mask; I feel like I'm in one of my nightmares, except this time, I'm the demon.

A moan of pain grabs our attention, and we all halt as one as Dorian lifts his chin toward the stairs to the dungeons. He got there faster than I thought he would in his condition. The need to survive is a funny thing.

We descend the stairs, and I decide it's time to make our presence known with a little song he used to make one of my nannies sing when I was due for a punishment.

"If you go down to the woods today, you're sure of a big surprise."

My voice comes out as an eerie tinkle, bouncing off the walls, echoing in the dungeon, making it even creepier.

"If you go down in the woods today, you'd better go in disguise."

We hear a moan of panic and a rattling of bars. All three of us grin, and I keep singing, moving deeper and deeper into the dark.

"For every bear there ever was,

will gather there for certain because,

today's the day the teddy bears have their picnic."

I yank open the wooden door to the dungeon entrance, giggling at the gargled cry that comes from inside. I see him at the end of the dank dungeon, desperately pulling at a barred gate that won't open. One arm is pulled out of its socket, blood dripping from gaping wounds, scars and bruises littering his flesh. I can see his muscles strain as he tries to get away, but the only other way out is the way we came in. So sad.

I put my arms behind my back, smiling widely and walking slowly on my tiptoes, swaying to the song.

"If you go down in the woods today, you'd better not go alone."

"It's lovely down in the woods today, but it's safer to stay at home."

"For every bear there ever was,

will gather there for certain because,

today's the day the teddy bears have their picnic."

I stand in front of him, tilting my head to the side with a grin. "Hi, Daddy."

I don't waste time on words. I don't tell him how much he fucked me up or how, when I was younger, all I wanted was for him to love me, to show me the tiniest amount of kindness. No words leave my lips as I bring the knife from behind my back and plunge it into his stomach.

He doesn't put up a fight, doesn't even try to stop me. He falls to the floor, and I crash to my knees, screaming as I sink the blade into him until he's no longer moving. Blood coats my face, dress, hair, everything until it's all I can see. I don't stop until my body aches in pain, leaving the knife embedded into his heart.

There will be no tears wasted on him, no more mourning who he should have been. His death is nothing, not even a blip in my story. *Nothing*.

"Goodbye, Daddy."

Two firm hands grab my shoulders, smoothing my hair, petting my head. I close my eyes, leaning into their touch, basking in their presence.

"How do you feel, pretty girl?"

I take a deep breath, staring at our father's limp, cold body, seeing the carnage I created, and I only feel one thing. "Free."

For so long, I've been terrified of him, scared he will take the two people I can't live without, and now, he's gone by my hand.

Bastian leans down, whispering in my ear. "Do you want to know how I feel?"

I chuckle, leaning my head back and closing my eyes. "I know how you feel."

Nothing turns Bas on more than blood—or the sight of me drenched in blood, it seems.

"Do you remember what I said I would do to you once you slaughtered our father?" Dorian asks, and something goes round my eyes, blocking my vision.

"Yes," I whisper, knowing what's about to happen, and having no problem with it.

I'm pushed on my hands and knees, my fingers gliding in the blood soaking the floor. My dress pushed up around my waist, and I feel the edge of a blade gliding across my skin.

"Do you know how much I want to cut up this pretty skin?" Dorian hisses, pushing the blade harder. "I want to mark your skin all over, see my scars coating your body for years to come. I want to carve my fucking name on every single inch."

The blade cuts into my thigh, and I gasp in pain but make no attempt to move away from it. I feel his tongue running up where he sliced me, catching my blood and groaning in ecstasy. He makes another cut and, this time, it feels deeper. My gasp turns into a cry, and my legs shake.

"Dorian," Bastian barks, and then there's silence. I don't know what's happening, but I don't dare move.

"It's okay. I'm fine," Dorian says, but I feel the cold knife press against my skin again.

"It wasn't you I was worried about, asshole," Bastian scoffs, but I can hear the tinge of worry in his voice.

The blade slices up again, but this time, it cuts my underwear and nothing else. He keeps slicing until I feel nothing covering me, and then I hear a clang as the knife drops to the ground. He runs his hands over my ass, dipping down between my legs, cupping my pussy.

"I want the whole dungeon to hear you scream as we fuck you," Dorian demands. "I want everyone in this hellhole to know exactly what's happening as we defile you, little sister."

He pushes two fingers inside me, and I moan loudly, pushing back on them.

"Every single person down here is for you, my pretty girl." Bastian runs his thumb over my bottom lip, and I open my mouth. "Everyone who helped that bastard take you from us is here—the ones who helped with transport, who forged documents, the sisters who withheld food, even the attendants who filled the car with petrol. They will all be punished for what they did to you."

I gasp at his words, moaning as Dorian adds another finger.

"You're soaked, angel. Does it turn you on knowing the depths our darkness takes us to when it comes to you?" Dorian asks, adding another finger, stretching me as far as I can go.

"Yes," I moan, tilting my head back, moving in time with the thrust of his fingers. I feel *so full.*

"There's nothing we wouldn't do for you," Bastian declares, forcing my mouth open, holding my cheeks.

"No one we wouldn't torture, wouldn't kill," Dorian continues, roughly taking his fingers away.

I hear dual zippers being undone, and Dorian runs the head of his cock along my slit, gathering my wetness, pressing against my entrance as Bastian runs the head of his against my lips, letting me taste the saltiness of his pre-cum, the metal balls of his piercing against my flesh.

"There has never been a moment on this Earth when you weren't mine, Octavia," Dorian whispers so softly, it brings tears to my eyes.

"I love you, my sweet, dark, twisted, pretty girl, and I'm going to fuck your throat until you're dragging your nails down my thighs, desperate for air."

Bastian forces his cock down my throat as soon as he finishes the sentence, and Dorian slams his dick into my pussy. They work in sync, not for a second being gentle. Bastian fists my hair and grabs the back of my neck, pushing his cock as far as it can go. I gag, spluttering, trying to breathe through my nose and swallow him down as much as I can. I run my tongue on the underside of his shaft and feel him shiver, gripping my hair tighter so I do it again.

Dorian snakes a hand around my waist, rubbing my clit as he angles his cock, grinding it over my g-spot. I moan around Bastian, pushing back on Dorian, making them both grunt in sync.

"Such a good fucking girl for us. My perfect angel," Dorian moans, and I keen at his praise, basking in it. "Fuck. Your cunt is perfect, squeezing my cock. I'm going to fill your pussy up, Octavia, brand you from inside with my cum."

I nod my head, muffling moans of agreement. Bastian chuckles, pulling out slightly so I can catch a breath. His thumb smooths my cheek lovingly, and a warmth builds in my stomach.

"Is our pretty girl going to cum on her big brother's cock?"

I nod, running my tongue over the piercings on the head of his cock, wishing I could stare at him, especially when he bucks his hips, moaning in pleasure.

"Fuck, do that again, baby."

I run my tongue over him, enjoying the way his hips stutter as I suck the head of his cock, flicking the piercing with the tip of my tongue.

"Holy fucking goddess," he moans, wrapping both of his hands around my head. "I'm going to come down your throat, and you're not going to swallow a single drop until I say."

I nod, letting him take over, flattening my tongue. Dorian picks up the pace, circling my clit, putting more pressure on it as his hips slam harder, his cock going deeper. My orgasm hits me fast and I cry out around Bastian, sucking him harder, hollowing my cheeks, my eyes rolling to the back of my head.

"Fuck, Octavia, that's it. Clamp that pussy around my cock," Dorian groans, bucking his hips a few more times before roaring his release.

Bastian comes at the same time, filling my mouth. My own orgasm carries on through it all, and I try my hardest to do as I'm told, not swallowing a drop. As soon as he releases my mouth, I take a deep breath in through my nose as Dorian keeps his cock inside me, running his hands soothingly down my thighs and over my ass.

"Open your mouth for me," Bastian orders, and I do as I'm told. Sticking my tongue out, I show him that I kept it all there.

I feel his breath on my face, his finger tracing through the mess on my tongue as he moans. A second later, his mouth latches onto my tongue, tasting his salty release. I move closer, fusing our lips together, letting him take what he wants.

He sucks my tongue and releases it with a pop, humming with pleasure. "Knew it. You even make my cum taste like honey with your sweetness, pretty girl."

I huff out a laugh, resting my head on his chest. "That's impossible, but I won't argue if it means you'll do that again."

"Did you like me sucking my cum from your tongue, tasting my own release?"

"She loved it if her soaking wet, pulsing cunt has anything to say about it." Dorian groans, slowly pulling out of me.

I feel a mixture of his cum and my own trickle down my thighs, but instead of him licking it up, I feel a soft cloth mopping up the mess. Probably just as well if he did that—I would need them again. I let them clean me up, basking in their soft touches, never wanting it to end. Once they're done, they manoeuvre me to my knees, undoing the blindfold.

"You know, you didn't need the blindfold. I would have liked to see you both while you were fucking me," I say, about to pull the mask off, but a hand grabs my wrist, stopping me.

"We know, but if you didn't have the blindfold, then you would have seen our masks a lot sooner than we wanted."

"What-"

I go to ask Dorien what the hell he means, but the words get stuck in my throat as I gaze up at them standing over me, kneeling on the floor. Masks cover their faces, the ones from my nightmares. I never described them before. Bastian is wearing the kiss me mask, Dorian the neon. My mouth hangs open in shock, and my head can't keep bouncing back and forth between the pair.

"What's the matter, pretty girl? Demon got your tongue?" Bastian lifts his mask up and winks, blowing me a kiss.

I scramble to my feet, staring at them. "But...how? They were nightmares; nothing in them was real. How do you know about the masks?"

"Were they nightmares, or were they an acid trip we sent you on once a month?" Dorian asks, lifting his mask to smirk before putting it back down.

"You were drugging me?"

No, they couldn't have been. They're messing with me for some weird reason.

"Drugged you. Chased you. Murdered people in front of you after we put these masks on them," Bastian lists off.

"Turned up without the masks to save you then comforted you when you came running after you *woke up*, promising we would keep you safe, just like in the nightmares. Only we can keep you safe, my dark angel."

Holy shit. Holy motherfucking shit. These unhinged, psychopathic, disturbed, fucked up motherfuckers.

"I am going to kill you," I seethe, twisting around and ripping the knife from my father's chest.

Bastian pushes Dorian violently to the side, laughing over his shoulder as he runs. "You owe me a free stab. I told you she would try to murder us." He cackles, running faster.

Dorian huffs, straightening his suit, but he quickly runs after Bastian, twisting his head back to me. His grey eyes flashing behind the neon blue crosses on the mask. "Come on, little sister. Your turn to chase us. The last one to get caught gets to take you on a date first."

"I'm not sure if either of you will be alive to take me on a blasted date," I shout, chasing after him.

He laughs so carefreely, it has me stopping in my tracks. I've never heard him laugh like that, not one moment in my life.

"That's my girl." He laughs again, and it sends a gigantic wave of warmth through me.

I shake my head, scowling, stomping my foot. "Stop trying to make me not want to kill you."

His laughter carries on, and I let a small smile pull at my lips, running after him.

21

OCTAVIA

I chase them throughout the castle, both staying in my sight the entire time but just out of reach. Bastian keeps trying to push Dorian to the ground or trip him up, but each time, Dorian snarls, straightening his suit before running again.

"I'm winning this date, fucker. I have it all planned and everything," Bastian whines, shouldering Dorian as they rush down the stairs.

"So do I, and we both know mine will be better than yours."

Dorian grabs the bannister, and instead of walking down the stairs, he jumps down to the platform landing. Bastian pauses, gasping in outrage.

"It will not! My date includes karaoke to Taylor Swift, and I'm finally ready to paint her nails. How the hell are you supposed to top that? Right, pretty girl?" He swings his head around, grinning at me as I reach the top of the stairs.

He's arranged a date with karaoke? They did that for me for my fifteenth birthday, set up the ballroom with pink streamers and a disco ball, glitter everywhere, with so many cupcakes that I got sick after trying to eat my way through them. Bastian and I were the only ones who did the karaoke, as Dorian point blank refused, but he sat and clapped, cheering me on while heckling Bastian.

I loved that birthday. I love all the birthdays they throw me. They always make them special and do something they know I would love, even if they hate it.

"Ha! Told you. She's speechless at my date plan, so you might as well give up now."

"In your nightmares. She just doesn't know what I've got planned yet."

"And what do you have planned, Rian?" I ask, twirling the blade in my hand.

"Catch Bastian first and find out, angel." Dorian smirks, licking his lips, eyeing me up in a way that has my legs trembling.

He runs again, and so do I. Bastian curses, trying to catch up and get further ahead. He jumps down the stairs, landing in the greeting hall a few seconds after Dorian. I pant, out of breath, on the second landing of the stairs. There's no way I can catch them; they're faster than me and know these halls better.

If I can't catch them, then I need to manipulate them.

I quickly untie the blood-stained ribbons on my legs, kicking off my shoes and climbing onto the bannister. It's luckily wide enough that I can balance easily, but the drop makes my stomach swirl.

"What are you doing, pretty girl?"

Bastian is the first to notice, looking over his shoulder as he stops running. Dorian twists, halting to a stop, his eyes widening as he sees me.

"Octavia," he barks, and I can't help giggling at the sternness of his tone.

I spin slowly to the side on the balls of my feet and walk across the bannister, holding out my arms for balance.

"I'm tired of chasing you, so I decided to change the game." I tip to the side, faking losing balance, and they both shout, rushing closer.

"Get down this very fucking second, Octavia, before you hurt yourself," Dorian orders, his eyes tracking my every movement.

I fake another slip, yelping, making sure I sound scared. They rush even closer, standing just below me in the perfect position.

"Well, if you insist, big brother." I smirk, letting my grin grow bigger, and jump right off the bannister.

"Motherfucking Christ, Octavia," Dorian shouts.

My stomach flips as I fall through the air, and for a single second, I wonder if I fucked up as I keep falling, but a few moments later, I feel their arms catch me. All three of us crash to the ground, their bodies protecting my fall.

They both groan as I lay over them, slightly winded. "Caught you both," I say, chucking the knife to the floor.

Bastian laughs, pulling me completely onto him, kissing me on the lips. "Fuck, I love you, my crazy girl."

"I love you too. Thanks for catching me."

"Always, baby. Always." He runs his nose across mine, and I close my eyes with a smile.

"Don't worry about me. I'm absolutely fine," Dorian grunts. I giggle, trying to pull myself out of Bastian's hold, but he locks his arms around my waist tighter.

"Share," he mutters, and Dorian scowls, snapping, "You're the one who's not sharing!"

He lunges for us, knocking Bastian on his back before laying on top of us, kissing me deeply. "Where's my thanks, angel?"

"I was getting there. You just didn't give me a chance."

He pulls back, raising his eyebrow, waiting expectantly. I huff out a laugh, shaking my head. "Thank you for saving me, Rian."

He cups my cheeks, resting his head on mine, staring deep into my eyes. "There will never be a time I don't save you."

The look he's giving me, the reverence in his tone, makes my heart thump wildly in my chest.

"I love you, Dorian. There will never be a time I don't love you."

"Octavia…" he whispers, his face scrunching up in frustration. I smooth out the creases with my thumb, cupping his cheeks.

"I know, Dorian. I don't need words, just you." Bastian clears his throat loudly, squeezing my waist harder as I lay on top of him. I roll my eyes, shaking my head. "Obviously I meant you too, Bas. I only need both of you."

"Just wanted to make sure the best one wasn't forgotten."

Dorian scoffs, pushing off me slightly. "Please. I'm the best, and we all know it."

"I think the fuck not."

Oh, I see where this is going, and I do not want to be in the middle while they tumble on the ground. "Guys," I try, but they ignore me.

Dorian lays back down on top of me and makes me lose my breath. They mutter at each other about who's the best, punching the other in the sides as I'm jolted to the side.

"Tell him I'm the best, pretty girl."

"No, tell him I'm the best. Who makes you come better, angel?"

"Uhhh. I am so not getting involved," I mutter, trying to get out from between them, but their focus shifts from each other to me.

"Come on, pretty girl. Be on my team." Bastian holds my sides, squeezing the spot I hate.

"Don't you dare," I snap, but I shouldn't have taken the bait.

"No, angel, be on my side," Dorian says tauntingly, grabbing my knees, about to squeeze.

"Don't fucking do it." I scowl, waiting, and they both act at the same time, tickling my worst spots.

Motherfuckers!

I laugh and scream, trying to kick and hit them as they continue their assault. I should not have dropped the knife; I could use it to stab them in the fucking dicks about now. I hate being tickled, and these bastards love to do it.

"Children, that behaviour will cease this moment," a cold, hard voice booms in the room, and all three of us stop moving immediately, my blood turning cold.

I know Dorian said he would be arriving, but I didn't think it would be today, and he's found all three of us on top of each other. I scramble to my feet, out of breath and horrified. Dorian and Bastian slowly rise, coming to either side of me. I want to take their hands for comfort, but I don't. I clasp them behind my back, ringing them nervously.

"Hello, Grandfather," I whisper, dropping into the customary curtsy that is expected when greeting him, staying in the position until he says, "Granddaughter."

I raise my head, meeting his ice grey eyes head on and holding in my shiver. He hasn't changed since the last time I saw him: grey, slicked back hair with a perfectly trimmed salt and pepper beard, wearing his signature bespoke grey suit. He looks nothing like the ones you see on tv shows. Nope, my grandfather looks like the head crime lord he is, and as he eyes the three of us, I've not forgotten the fear he instils.

"Grandfather," Dorian and Bastian say, giving curt nods, not bowing like expected or waiting for him to greet them.

"You're early," Dorian states with an accusatory tone that has me sucking in a deep breath.

Grandfather purses his lips, eyeing Dorian with an expression I can't decipher. He takes a few steps towards us, and I hold my breath, straightening my spine.

"Yes, well, we have other things to discuss, apart from your missing father." He speaks to Dorian but doesn't take his eyes off me, taking in my blood-stained pink dress.

"And what might that be?" Dorian asks, taking a step in front of me, blocking his view as I feel Bastian slide around to stand at my back.

Grandfather hums, taking a small step back, studying the three of us. I peek out from behind Dorian, catching our grandfather frowning before Bastian pulls me back.

"I've arranged a marriage for your sister. Her intended will be arriving soon, and I wanted to get a start on the plans before that happened, seeing as it will be outside the bloodline."

My heart sinks, a cold sweat breaking out all over my body as bile rises in my throat.

No.

Bastian snarls as Dorian grows still, his head snapping up. Bastian's arm circles my waist in a vice grip, and I search for his and Dorian's hands, unable to stop myself. They each grab one, holding me as tight as I hold them.

"I think you need to change your plans and find a new bride, old man," Bastian snaps.

Grandfather tilts his head, a mocking smirk playing at his lips. "Why would I need to find a new bride when your sister is perfectly able to fulfil that role?"

Dorian takes a step back, standing at my side, and I do my best to keep the fear from my face.

"Because you are talking about our wife," Dorian says, making him eye the three of us more closely. "We may share with each other, but no one else."

"Is that so?" he says, rubbing his beard, raising an eyebrow.

"Fucking try taking her and see what happens," Bastian snarls, flattening his hand on my stomach, resting his chin on my shoulder, biting my neck until a small groan escapes me. "No one else has survived thus far. Do you really think you'll be the exception?"

He says nothing for a few seconds, simply staring in silence before slowly walking into my space, towering over me. He grasps my chin quickly, pinching it between his fingers in a punishing grip, making me hiss as he tilts my head up. Dorian and Bastian snarl, but I squeeze their hands, digging my nails in to stop them from doing anything that will get us killed.

"Is this how you want to play it, Octavia? Are you happy to hide behind your brothers instead of doing what the bloodline demands of you? What *I* demand of you?"

I hold his stare, refusing to cower. I just murdered my own father, stabbed him until I could no longer raise the knife. I will not run away scared now.

"You heard my husbands: try taking me," I whisper. "I dare you."

The seconds tick on slowly as he decides what to do, and I don't think I breathe the entire time. He finally lets go of my chin, taking a step back, gazing at the three of us in disgust.

"I will not stand here and have this conversation with you like common people in a greeting hall. Clean yourself up, and we will continue during dinner. Ramsey," he barks, clicking his fingers, and his personal butler who travels with him pops out from nowhere.

"Yes, my lord."

"Please ensure dinner is ready in two hours. My *grandchildren* need to clean up." He dismisses us with a wave of his hand as he turns his back and leaves.

"Of course, my lord." Ramsey bows deeply at Grandfather's retreating back, making his way to the kitchen.

I'm frozen in my spot, unable to move or even blink. I just stood up to Vincent Stone. I'm a dead woman walking.

"Take her to our room and get ready. I need to sort out a few things, but I'll meet you there before we have to go down," Dorian whispers to Bastian, and it brings me out of my meltdown.

"Where are you going?" I ask in a panic, tugging at the hand still encased in mine.

He uncurls my fingers, giving me a quick kiss and brushing my hair out of my face. "I'm not going anywhere, angel. Just sorting a few things out for dinner. Go with Bastian and shower. I'll be there before you know it."

"Dorian," I whisper as he pulls away.

"It's all going to be okay. I promise." He kisses my head before dashing off, but I don't see where he's going as Bastian scoops me up in his arms. I press my face into his chest, soaking up the comfort he gives me.

"I've got you, pretty girl. I've always got you."

22

OCTAVIA

Water pours down over my head, washing away the blood of my father, taking away one of my sins, leaving me sparkling clean. Bastian finishes washing my hair, gently running his fingers through the strands, getting out the knots.

He turns off the shower when I don't move, wrapping me in a fluffy, warm towel, guiding me into his room. Everything has been fixed from my destruction, and apart from the new furniture, it's like nothing happened.

He sits me on the bed, squatting in front of me in a towel of his own, cupping my cheek. "How are you doing, pretty girl?"

Isn't that a loaded question? I murdered our father, found out it was my brothers who were the masked demons haunting my nightmares—but they weren't actually nightmares, an acid trip instead. Then, our grandfather turned up to declare I'll be wed to someone outside of the bloodline. That in itself is enough to send me over the edge, because hardly anyone marries outside of the bloodline.

Bastian moves his hand to my thighs, and I hiss, remembering the cut Dorian left there. I move the towel to examine it and see that nothing needs to be done. It's a shallow cut, no stitches needed, but it's a memory all the same.

"What was that about down in the dungeon?" I ask, lifting my head to meet his gaze. "You sounded worried when you barked Dorian's name while he was doing this."

Bas huffs, twisting his lips, but it doesn't take him long to cave and let me avoid the question. He stands up, dropping his towel, showing off his beautiful, tattooed body.

"Dorian did every single one of these," he says, running his fingers over the tattoo above his cock that says *kiss me*. Really, I should have connected the dots when I saw that one. "Except this one. I did this myself."

He gives me a dirty smirk, biting his bottom lip as I roll my eyes, slapping his hand away.

"Yeah, I get why you would have done that one. Now, back to explaining the rest."

"Boo. No fun." He sticks out his tongue but carries on, turning around so I can see his back, and I notice for the first time my name alongside Dorian's on his ass.

"Our dear brother has a tiny obsession with marking what he thinks belongs to him. You won't believe the number of times I woke up to him standing over me with a knife, just staring, not blinking."

"Seriously?" I ask, a burst of laughter breaking free.

"Dead serious," he says, twisting his head over his shoulder. "And that's what I thought I would be when I was younger. Thought my deranged twin wanted to murder me, but no, he just wanted to carve my skin up so I knew I belonged to him."

He rolls his eyes as he turns back, and I stand, tracing each one of his tattoos on his chest. He shivers at my touch, watching me intently.

"He drunkenly told me once about his craving, let me in on his little secret. I thought about it for hours afterwards. I was going to give in and let him carve me up like a turkey if that's what he needed, but then, the thought of tattoos came to me. He practised for a while, wanting to be perfect. The first one he gave me was your name."

He pulls me to him, and I wrap my arms around his waist, leaning my cheek on his chest. His fingers go back to my hair, soothing me like he did in the shower. "That one is my favourite."

I close my eyes tight, my thoughts swirling, ones I've tried not to think about.

"I'm going to lose you," I whisper, tears falling down my cheeks.

It's the one thing I've dreaded all my life, the thing that has terrified me more than my fucked-up family, and now, it's happening.

"The fuck you are," Bastian snaps.

"Do you honestly think there is anything or anyone on this Earth who can take you from us, Octavia?"

Dorian storms into the room and grasps my hair tight, tilting my head up as he looms over me, still in Bastian's arms.

"Well, Octavia? Do you?" He shakes, rage flashing in his gaze, and it fuels my own as I rip myself from between them.

"It's not that simple!"

"Of course it's that simple," Bastian scoffs, carefree as always, like everything is just a game.

"No, it's not," I shout, stamping my foot. "If we go against Grand-father, he could slaughter us. There will be no quick and easy death. I witnessed what he does to people, and calling him the devil would be cruel to the devil. He's the head of the elders, the leader of this whole fucking bloodline."

My voice shakes as they try to step towards me, try to pull me into their embrace so they can make me believe we're not fucked, that everything is okay. I push them away, shaking my head.

"If you go up against him, Dorian, you will lose everything. If by some miracle he decides not to kill us, everything you have worked for in the bloodline..." My throat closes as tears roll down my cheeks. "I won't be the reason for your downfall. I won't let our twisted love destroy everything."

I was foolish thinking I could have them the way I want. I ignored all the consequences outside of this castle. The bloodline will never let us be together; our *grandfather* won't allow it, especially if he has plans for me.

"I've been so stupid," I mutter, the tears rolling faster, my heart shattering.

A foolish girl with toxic dreams would never get her happy ending.

"If loving you causes our downfall, then we will burn the world as we dance in the ashes," Dorian declares, yanking me towards him and forcing his lips on mine.

My head spins as he kisses me, taking my breath away, making the world turn.

"I fucking love you, Octavia. My world doesn't make sense when you're not around. Everything is black and grey, but when you're with me, it shines in blinding colour. I always wanted to pull you into the dark, but no matter where you go, you shine so fucking bright."

He breathes harshly against my lips, and I shake in his arms.

"You are ours. Nothing can take you from us, not even you. Don't make me chain you to me to prove that, because I will."

He stares deep into my eyes, and I feel the truth in every single word he says. No one can take me from them, and I have to trust them.

He said he loved me.

"I want you to carve your name into my skin," I whisper against his lips, and he sucks in a deep breath.

He gave me something special, something I don't think either of us thought he could give me. I want to give him something in return.

He picks me up, digging his fingers into my thighs, rushing forward and slamming my back into the wall as he devours my mouth. I wrap my hands around his neck, squeezing as tight as I can to cut off his breathing. He moans, grinding his hardening cock against my bare pussy.

"I'm going to carve your skin up so prettily, angel," he mutters, biting my bottom lip until it bleeds. "I'm going to fucking brand you as mine."

"If I let you carve up my pretty skin, will you tell me you love me as well?" Bastian smirks at our side.

Dorian breaks the kiss, scowling at Bastian as he leans against the wall, wiggling his eyebrows. "I'll carve my fucking dick on your forehead, you moment breaking bastard."

I laugh loudly, shaking my head as Dorian drops me to my feet. "Go put on the prettiest dress you have, angel. We haven't got long."

I nod my head, sucking in a deep breath, some nerves filtering back in.

"It will all be okay, pretty girl. Trust us." Bastian wipes away the tears on my face, kissing my head.

"Always," I whisper, leaving their room to get ready.

23

DORIAN

Octavia steps out of her room, her heels clicking on the floor, gazing at us with her wide doe eyes that set my heart on fire. I wondered if she was going to stick to the bloodline guidance and wear one of her old dresses for our meal, but she does my toxic soul proud by wearing a floor length white gown tight to her body, showcasing every curve, covered in crystals, leaving one arm bare while the over is covered by a sleeve, a long slit revealing her thick thigh, body shimmer making the stretch-marks there sparkle. Her white-blonde hair is slightly curled, pulled over her bare shoulder.

"I've never seen you look more like an angel," I whisper, capturing her face, sucking her bottom lip into my mouth and tasting her light pink lipstick.

She moans, melting at my touch as easily as breathing. I always knew I owned her, never doubted for a second that she was mine, but I never realised how much I was hers. Love isn't something I ever considered when I thought of her. She was my possession, my property; no one was going to take what was mine away from me, but I missed the moment she claimed me right back, when she took me as hers.

I have fallen sickeningly, obsessively in love with this woman, something I never believed myself capable of, and I wouldn't change a thing.

"My turn," Bastian snaps, barging into my shoulder, stealing her out of my grasp.

He twirls her in a circle, making her giggle before bending her dramatically and going in for a romantic movie kiss. She still giggles against his lips as she kisses him, melting into his touch as much as she did mine.

That is why we work so well, why my brother and I are not complete without the other. I cannot give her that, the carefree, playful kind of love. No matter how unhinged and damaged my brother is, he can be completely free. His scars and torment mean he doesn't have a single care in the fucking world. My damage is different. I need to control, I'm too possessive. I can give them safety and peace to just be.

My sweet Octavia is more damaged than both of us, just in a different way. She craves to be loved, to be cherished, to have everything she so desperately wanted all her life and could only get from us, but it was tainted with fear of everything else. I plan to slaughter every possible thing that could bring that fear back, anything that takes away from her happiness. I might not be able to give her sweet romance, but I *can* give her my fucking life for her to do with as she pleases.

"Time to go now, kids," I say, snapping my pocket watch closed. Dinner is about to be served, and this is a meal I do not want to be late for.

"What have you got planned?" Octavia asks, frowning at me as Bastian sets her on her feet.

"Whatever do you mean?" I shrug my shoulder, trying to school my face into a neutral expression, but I can't help the smirk still pulling at my lips.

"Oh, you've done something extremely fucked up." Bastian bounces on the balls of his feet, his eyes sparkling with bloodthirsty excitement. "I know that look. You're giving the same look you did when you made Octavia's nanny eat her husband's heart by making her think it was a cow's. She got about halfway through before you dumped his body on the table with his chest caved in."

Bastian laughs hysterically, holding his stomach, as Octavia's eyes widen, her head whipping between the two of us.

"I'm sorry, what?" she exclaims. "When did you do this?"

I don't need long to remember. I know the exact date. "Fourteen years, seven months, and nine days ago, give or take a few hours."

A burst of nervous laughter erupts from her as she shakes her head in bewilderment. "A memorable event, then."

I step towards her, trailing my fingers through her luscious hair. "Of course it was. It was the day after she cut your hair against your will at Father's request. Bastian and I had put semi permanent pink dye on the ends because you wanted to look like a fairy princess."

I brush my lips over her forehead, inhaling her sweet scent of strawberries. "Like I was ever going to let that go unpunished. Every fairy princess needs her demons."

"I cut off some of her toes and then made her wear them as a necklace," Bastian adds, snaking his arm around her waist from the side, placing his lips on her hand right next to mine. "I still have it somewhere if you want it."

"I think I'll pass on that." She pulls away, scrunching up her nose. Don't blame her on that front. "In terms of jewellery, I'll stick with platinum, maybe some silver, but never toes, Bas. Never toes."

Bastian tilts his head, shaking it from side to side. "Fingers?"

Octavia rears back, and I close my eyes, counting to ten.

"No, Bastian. No body parts of any kind."

"What about my cum? I've seen a shop online that dries it out and puts it into jewellery. They look so pretty, and it would match this outfit perfectly," he counters, trying desperately for some inane reason to get her to agree to it.

She sighs heavily, her foot tapping on the ground. "You've already got it, haven't you?"

My eyes fly open, and I stare at Bastian's guilty face. His cheeks turn red, and he scuffs his boot on the ground, letting go of her waist, shoving his hands in his black jean pockets.

"No," he mutters, and that is definitely a yes.

"Bastian?" she says, trying to get him to look at her.

"I said no. That would be a stupid gift to get someone." He forces a laugh, staring intently at the floor, scuffing his shoes.

Octavia runs her fingers through his beard, forcing him to look at her as she softens her voice. "I would love a necklace made from your...cum."

"Really?"

His head snaps up, a big wild smile on his face that proves infectious. I can't help the little smirk on my own, and it grows wider as he pulls the necklace from his pocket.

"A pearl necklace." I chuckle, and he scowls, pulling it closer to his chest, hiding it.

Octavia frowns at me over her shoulder, giving me the evil eye. "It's beautiful, Bastian. I love it," she says, giving him her full focus. I let them have their moment, moving over to the door, leaning against the frame.

"You like it?" he asks with all the hopes of a puppy dog wanting attention from its owner.

"I love it. Put it on me?"

She turns around, lifting her hair, waiting for him to clasp the necklace around her neck. It is quite pretty—a small delicate gold chain with a single round pearl that rests in the centre of her chest.

She twirls the pearl between her fingers with a warm smile as she gazes up at him with so much love in her eyes that I feel it in my gut.

I take a step towards them, clearing my throat, feeling like a total bastard having to put a stop to their moment, but time is ticking on. "We need to go, sweetheart."

Bastian raises her chin with two of his fingers, placing a soft kiss on his lips before taking her hand.

"Okay, sugar tits, let's get the show on the road." He winks, sending me a kiss, but I don't take the bait. With Bastian, you have to know which battles are worth it and which ones aren't.

Octavia reaches for my hand as we leave, squeezing tight, her nails digging into my skin. "It's all going to be okay, angel."

I've made sure of it.

Grandfather is already waiting for us, sitting in our father's spot at the dining table, taking a sip of scotch. He swirls the amber liquor in the crystal glass, raising an eyebrow at the three of us.

"You're late." His voice booms in the room, echoing off the walls, his tone low and scolding. He's trying to make us feel ashamed, but it's been a long time since any of us were children.

Waiters flurry in with plates of food, placing them expertly on the fully decorated table with the best black lining and silverware, dahlias as the centrepiece as I instructed. Grandfather's favourite.

"It seems we are right on time," I say, directing Octavia and Bastian to our seats.

The moonlight shines through the large windows, stars twinkling in the sky: the perfect night for the final pieces to fall into place.

I had every seat at the table removed, leaving only the two chairs at opposing ends, one having two flanking it on each side. Octavia sits on my right, Bastian on my left. I can tell by the twitch of his hand when he releases her that he doesn't want to be on the opposite side, but he doesn't say anything.

"Interesting gown choice, Granddaughter."

Octavia takes a sip of her wine, taking her sweet ass time. She sets her glass down and turns to me. "What's being served tonight?"

Bastian lets out a quick burst of laughter, and I have to tamp down my own, hiding my smirk. Grandfather bristles, slamming his glass on the table, but we all ignore him.

"Veal is being served tonight, angel." Her lips turn down, grimacing in disgust. "Don't worry, I've already asked them to make you a different dish. I believe Chef was going to prepare you some pasta," I tell her, making her frown turn into a smile.

More waiters enter, placing a covered plate in front of each of us, removing the top with a flourish to reveal the meal. Octavia groans, leaning down to smell her creamy pasta, making the most delicious sound that has my cock hardening. I shift in my seat, catching Bastian out of the corner of my eye doing the same.

"I have not come to be ignored," Grandfather snaps, grabbing his knife and fork, cutting violently into his veal. "Leave us," he barks at the staff, and they scuttle away quickly.

Octavia twirls a bit of pasta on her fork, gazing up from her eyelashes, pursing her lips. "I'm sorry, Grandfather. I didn't realise there was a question in that statement. *Was* there a question you wanted to ask about my gown?"

Bastian pauses with his drink midway to his lips, as stunned as I am at her retort. My angel has grown her talons. We wait to see what he'll do, if his anger will rise and cause a scene, or if he will try the sugar sweet poison that he likes to lure people in with.

Turns out, it's neither. He takes a bite out of his meat, humming at the taste. Octavia turns back to her food with a small, prideful smile, and I grasp her thigh, giving it a squeeze. We eat in silence for a few minutes. Bastian only takes a couple bites of the meat before turning his nose up at it, trying to steal Octavia's pasta. I personally find it very delectable, but I think that has more to do with where I got it.

"How long have you been involved with your brothers, Octavia?" Grandfather asks, leaning back in his chair. "Or would you prefer I call them your boyfriends? They are certainly not your husbands, seeing as there have been no legal proceedings."

She shrugs her shoulders, batting Bastian's fork away as he goes in for another piece, rolling her eyes. "Either is fine."

He opens his mouth to no doubt scold her, but I cut in, stopping whatever vile words were about to spew out.

"The legal proceedings will happen in the autumn, as per my *little sister's* request." I smirk watching him grimace in distaste.

"*The wedding*," he says, clutching his cutlery tight, "will take place in a month's time, and it will be with the groom I've arranged. I planned to discuss it with your father before he went missing. I knew Octavia was sent away to correct her behaviour, and I thought this wedding would be a perfect permanent solution that wouldn't put a stain on the Stone name."

He sneers at her, cutting roughly into his meat, taking a big swig of drink to wash it down. Sweat starts to shine just slightly on his forehead, and he pulls at the neck of his shirt, loosening his tie.

"The only reason I did not stand in your way bringing her back was because I needed her to return. Don't think I didn't know all about your scheming to bring your sister home and everyone you killed in the process. Don't think-" He sputters, his sentence cut off as he coughs violently.

Octavia stops eating, and Bastian stops trying to steal her food, both of them shifting their focus to our grandfather. I lean back in my chair, taking another bite, savouring the surprisingly sweet taste.

"And don't think I didn't plan exactly for that." I smirk, grabbing my glass, swirling the amber liquid.

"What...what is the meaning of this?" Grandfather coughs, grabbing his handkerchief. Blood splutters from his lips; it's only a few speckles, but it will certainly be more extensive in a few more minutes.

"What's happening?" He stands up from his chair, or at least tries to, before falling back down, his limbs growing weak. "Ramsey," he bellows, as predictable as ever.

The door swings open, and Ghost walks through instead, carrying a silver serving tray with Ramsey's head perfectly displayed on a bed of salad, an apple between his teeth.

"Jesus," Octavia mutters under her breath, shaking her head.

Bastian smirks, keeping his gaze on our grandfather, not letting him out of his sight—just in case. He already knows the plan.

"Oh no, poor Ramsey seems to have had a minor accident," Bastian says, putting his elbows on the table, resting his chin on his hands, pouting. "Guess that means no one was able to taste your food or drink. Huh, I sure hope no one did anything to it."

"You stupid boys," Grandfather wheezes, more sweat dripping down his head as he undoes his tie completely. "You are children playing a grown-up game. Ramsey isn't...the only one I have in the manor."

His eyes flick to Ghost, a smug smile on his face that falters as he places Ramsey's head in front of him and walks away, right out the door.

"Ghost! Ghost, come back here this moment." He bangs his fist on the table and hunches over in another coughing fit.

I take the moment to grab Octavia's hand, an uncomfortable feeling settling in my stomach at the revelation I have to give next. I didn't want her to find out; I planned on dealing with him alone so she would never know. I allowed a single flaw into my plan at him arriving early, and I will pay for that.

"I'm sorry about this part, angel. Forgive me."

She gazes at me with a bewildered look, her brows pulling together, scrunching up her little nose. "For what?"

I don't have time to break it easy to her. Time is ticking on, and the poison is working fast. I stand up, nodding my head to Bastian for him to take over. He rushes round and pulls her up until he can hold her in his arms.

"Did it never occur to you why Ghost volunteered so readily to be your spy in this castle? He was in the ranks to be a top player, and he left it all to do this. Doesn't make sense, does it?"

I crouch down beside him, pushing him back in his chair, lifting his head. "He's Octavia's biological father. He's been working with me since the moment he came here. Lucinda was already pregnant before she married Father, something he found out quickly but decided to save face than admit it. You would have murdered him had you known, and that privilege belonged to my sweet sister."

I twist my head and catch the heartbroken gaze on Octavia's face as she leans into Bastian's arms. I'll make it up to her. I'll do anything.

"How does he taste, by the way?" I ask Grandfather, turning my attention back to him. "I found him surprisingly sweet. I thought it would be bitter, seeing how much of a bastard he was."

He wheezes in the chair, the poison seeping through his veins, blood trickling out of the corner of his mouth. His eyes flick to his plate, gazing at the slab of meat he thought was veal but turned out to be his son.

I reach into my pocket, producing a needle with the antidote. His fingers wiggle, arm falling as he tries to reach for it.

"Ah, ah," I tut. "Not yet." I grab a chair, pulling it closer to him, twirling the thing that may very well save his life between my fingers.

"I will give you this antidote, Grandfather. I'm not a monster. Well, I am, but I'm a cunning one," I say, leaning back and crossing my legs. "Your death will bring me nothing but work. I'm not in the mood to rule the bloodline yet, not when I've just gotten Octavia back. I want to give her the world, let her have some fun for once in her life, but make no mistake: I *will* be coming for your blood one day. It just doesn't have to be today."

I will run the bloodline one day, as I was fucking made to. I thrive in the darkness, lost in the shadows, pulling the strings of everyone around me. I will do it now if I need to, but I meant what I said. I want to give Octavia some peace, some fun. If he declines, Bastian can be that for her, but I want to be as well.

"What...do...you...want?" he gasps, slumped in his chair.

I lean forward, grasping his chin, pulling his head so he really hears me. "What I want is a blood promise that nothing will ever happen to Octavia. She will no longer answer to the bloodline; she is free from it. You will give your blessing to our marriage, Bastian and I will take our father's place in the bloodline, and we will work as normal with the freedom to accept or decline jobs. We will receive immunity for almost killing you, and it will be a secret no one else will know about. No one will know how easy it was to take you from your throne."

I place the syringe by his heart, raising an eyebrow, waiting. He licks his bloodstained lips, his gaze flickering down to it, then back up. I shrug my shoulder, lowering the needle, but he takes the last of his strength to grab my wrist, stopping me.

"Deal," he croaks, and I slam the syringe straight into his heart. He bellows, his scream of pain echoing in the room before he slumps in his chair.

I leave it sticking out of his chest and walk back over to Octavia and Bastian. The latter stares at our grandfather with pure, unhinged joy, the former staring at me with pure anger.

"Angel," I say, but her head whips around, eyes flaring with accusation.

"Later," she snaps, leaving no room for argument, shrugging out of Bastian's hold. She stomps over to her chair, pulling it out roughly, plopping down, and downing the rest of her drink.

Bastian winces, and we share a look, knowing we are going to have to do some major grovelling to make up for keeping that from her.

Grandfather groans, pulling the needle out of his chest and placing it on the table. He grabs a napkin, wiping his mouth and face, shaking his head. Bastian prods the meat on his plate, scrunching up his nose, and Octavia watches him making the same face.

"Was it the food or the drink?" Grandfather says, his voice raspy.

I smirk, watching as he eyes the two things as I shake my head. "Your cutlery. It was bathed in poison, and the remnants soaked into your skin."

I click my fingers, and a maid comes in carrying a new, poison free set of cutlery, handing it to him. He eyes it for a moment, but only for a few seconds before he takes it. He keeps his gaze on me, cutting into the meat on his plate, chewing slowly. Not to be outdone, I do the same.

"At least your father was good for something. He makes a fine tender piece of meat," he says, taking a sip of his drink.

"I think I'm going to vomit," Octavia whispers, her complexion slightly green. I try to grab her leg to soothe her, but she bats my hand away.

"What date did you plan for the wedding, then? The invites will need to go out, events arranged. I'm sure I can find another bride the Carters will find suitable; they did love the picture of Octavia, but no matter. Will you be telling the bloodline about her true paternity?" Grandfather asks, all civil and polite. You would never guess from his tone that he was seconds away from dying by our hand.

"No," Bastian and I say at the same time. We don't care what anyone thinks.

"Very well." He nods, snapping his fingers for his drink to be re-filled. "I know you'll be coming for me now, Dorian. It won't be this easy ever again."

I smirk, raising my glass, taking a sip before saying, "Yes, but like this time, you'll never see me coming, and there will be no escape."

24

BASTIAN

The silence is driving me crazy. I'm itching under my skin, desperate to break it, but every time I open my mouth, Dorian shoots me a scolding frown, shaking his head. This all his stupid fault; he didn't need to mention that Ghost was Octavia's bio daddy. He just can't help himself; he needs them to know how much he fucked them. Except this time, he's fucked us both in the process.

Octavia opens our bedroom door, kicking off her shoes and unzipping her dress, letting it pool onto the floor. My mouth waters at the sight of her pale skin shimmering in the light, our marks all over her skin, a white corset clinging to her body with sexy as fuck lace booty shorts that show off the bottom half of her plump ass. Goddamn, I want to take a bite out of it.

She walks over to my bedside cabinet, rifling through my drawers, hunting for something. I glance at Dorian, and neither of us seems to know what's going on. I expected anger, bloodshed, maybe a few tears. I could handle that; I would know what to do with that. Let her stab and hit the fuck out of me. I'd sit there and take it until she exerted herself, and then I'd bend her over, sinking my dick into her dripping wet pussy, making her scream as she couldn't stop coming around my cock.

This silence is weird. I don't like it.

"Gotcha," she mutters, finding whatever it was she was looking for.

She rushes towards us with a knife, and I let out a sigh of relief. Finally, she'll get her anger out. I push Dorian forward, sacrificing him to the worst of the violence. I want the horny rage, not the actual murder.

He braces himself, waiting for her to plunge it into his flesh, not trying to stop or block it, knowing he deserves it. But instead of stabbing him, she flips the knife around in her hand, giving him the handle.

"Angel?" he questions, his forehead pinched together.

"You're supposed to stab with the pointy end, pretty girl," I say, giving her valuable instructions, even though I taught her that one when she was five years old.

She rolls her eyes, shaking her hand as she places the knife in Dorian's hand. "I know what end to stab with, Bas, but I'm not the one doing the carving tonight."

What is going on? She doesn't want to kill us?

Dorian's eyes flash, and his hand shakes as he takes it from her. I see the blood rushing through his body, turning his skin pink, the adrenaline and temptation of finally being able to do what he truly craves taking over his rational thinking.

For fuck's sake. I never have to be the damn rational one.

"Do you maybe want to talk about what happened, what you found out? I know you promised this to him, but Dorian will understand not doing it tonight, waiting until you're ready."

I smack him in the ribs when he says nothing, clutching the knife harder in his hand, so mesmerised that I wouldn't be surprised if I saw actual stars in his eyes.

"Would you, brother?" I hiss.

He thankfully blinks out of his state, coming back into the room, shaking his head. "We don't have to do this tonight, angel. Let's talk about everything. I'm sorry for it coming out-"

She slaps her hand on his mouth, smothering the words.

"I don't want to talk about it. I don't want to even think about it. We just survived Vincent Stone, we have permission to get married, and you have both told me you loved me." Her voice cracks as she shakes her head. "I don't want to think of anything except what we planned to do when we got back to this room."

"You—" She points to me, crooking her finger, pulling me towards her on an invisible string as my feet move of their own accord. "You are going to get down on your knees and eat my pussy so fucking well, I'm in danger of passing out."

"Yes fucking ma'am," I growl, my dick hard as stone in seconds.

"And you." She turns her head to Dorian, releasing her hand from his mouth. "You are going to select a piece of my body to carve your name into, and then the both of you are going to fuck me until I actually pass out. You are going to show me how much you fucking love me, how much you want me."

"Yes, angel," Dorian says softly, gazing into her eyes, checking that this is what she needs as I do the same.

I can't see any doubt, any inclination that this isn't what she wants, and as she stares right back at us, I can see a trickle of anger working in that we're not doing anything.

"Now," she barks, and I swear, I almost come.

I groan in pure fucking pleasure at her command, wanting her to take charge. Dorian moves, but I move quicker, scoping her up in my arms, rushing to our new bed. I chuck us both into it, diving on top of her, burying my face between her breasts. She softly giggles, running her hands through my hair, pushing my face deeper. Fuck, I would happily suffocate to death between these.

I drag my tongue over her bare flesh, and she arches into my touch, a sweet moan ripping from her lips.

"Knife," I bark, holding out my hand.

Dorian drops it into my palm, and I trace the edge of the blade up Octavia's side. She stills, letting me put pressure on it. The further down the knife goes, the higher I rise until I'm hovering over her on my knees, the knife at the bottom of her corset. The blade cuts through the fabric easily, the ripping sound like music to my ears.

As soon as her breasts are uncovered, I blindly chuck the knife back to Dorian, taking one of her nipples into my mouth, swirling my tongue around the hardening bud, giving the same attention to the other once I'm done. Her back arches more, throwing her head back, a beautiful whimper coming from her as I bite down until I taste blood.

"Always such a good girl for her big brothers," Dorian says, standing by her head, running his fingers through her hair. "Do you know how much your brothers love you?"

I slowly kiss down her stomach, tracing patterns with my tongue, making sure I get every inch of her. She shakes her head no, gazing at him with wide, vulnerable eyes. He bends down, placing his nose on hers, getting that soft look he only gives her.

"You're ours, Octavia. We want to consume you, to fucking devour you. There has never been anyone else for us. You own our hearts, our fucking souls. We are living and breathing monsters, but we are your monsters."

She sucks in a deep breath, shaking at his words and our touch. I place myself between her legs, dragging my tongue slowly up her slit, tasting how fucking wet she is. "We are damned and damaged. There is no salvation for us, but there will never be anything or anyone more important to us than you. Be our shining light in a world of darkness, pretty girl."

Dorian fists her hair, lifting her head so she can gaze at me. She nods slowly, licking her lips. "Always."

I suck her clit between my lips, flicking the bundle of nerves with my tongue, watching her eyes roll to the back of her head, Dorian still fisting her hair. He captures her mouth, swallowing her moan, claiming her in a way that has me rubbing my dick on the bed. I fucking love it when he gets possessive of her, and it turns me on when he gets all possessive of me. The need to be wanted ignites a fire in my veins that will have me doing anything to get it.

Some people might resent the way they were brought up if they were in my shoes, and they wouldn't be wrong to feel that way. It's a fucked-up life, but I wouldn't change a thing, because it got me them. I would live through it all again, take every beating, every moment I thought my life was about to end, every single action that turned me into the monster I am today, I would do it again and again if the results were me having her.

There has not been one moment in my life that I didn't love her with so much obsession that I thought my heart would tear to shreds.

"That's it, angel. Come on his face. Drowning him in your cum so I can lick it off and have a taste for myself," Dorian husks.

Octavia whines, rolling her hips, thrusting against my mouth. I slip three fingers into her sweet pussy, curling them to catch the spot inside that makes her squirt, burying my face into her pussy, my nose brushing against her soft blonde curls. I flatten my tongue on her clit, pushing down hard, knowing she needs the pressure. She cries out, her hands flying to my head, holding me in place.

"You're such a beautiful wreck for us; so broken, so shattered. We weren't supposed to fit together, Octavia," Dorian whispers, dragging the knife down her chest, circling her nipples. "We were never meant to be, but we claimed you the second you were born. We didn't know then what you would be to us; we just knew that you belonged to us. So, we helped collect all the pieces they shattered and forged them into ones that would fit with ours. We melded ours to be what *you* needed. You fucking own us, Octavia Stone. Don't you ever doubt that."

She shudders at his words, goosebumps raising up on her skin. Dorian keeps dragging the knife down until he reaches the top of her thigh, humming in approval, selecting the spot for his name right next to my face.

He nicks the top of her thigh right by her groin, making a cut on my cheek at the same time. He leans down, running his tongue along the shallow cut, licking up the droplets of blood that bubble there. I feel his breath on my cheek as he keeps going, running his tongue up my cheek to lick the wound. I groan into Octavia's pussy, sinking my face deeper, my cock throbbing.

His lips trace across my ear, a deep, dark chuckle rumbling in his chest. "Your blood tastes almost as sweet as hers, little brother. After I carve her, I'm going to put my fucking mark on you."

I shudder at the possession in his tone, letting the twisted feelings I have for my twin roll through me. I don't want him like I want her, but I want to feel owned, and these two are the only ones I will ever let own me.

Octavia pants, raising up on her arms, gazing down at us with her pupils blown. I smirk against her pussy, slowly pumping my fingers, dragging my tongue up and down her slit.

"Do you like that, pretty girl? Do you want our big brother to mark me as his, just like you?"

Her pouty mouth pops open, and she rolls her hips in time with my movements, nodding her head. "Yes," she says, biting her bottom lip.

"Well," I say, nipping at the flesh on her thigh where Dorian is going to mark her. "If that's what my little sister wants, that's what she gets. Always."

Her eyes sparkle, the soft smile appearing that I fucking adore. "Thank you, big brother."

I groan, sucking her clit back between my lips, carrying on with my mission to make her squirt all over my face. I fucking love it when she calls me that.

Dorian holds her thigh with one hand, and I help, clasping it tight, making sure she doesn't wriggle too much while he does it. His cock is rock hard in his trousers as he makes the first letter, his breath heavy, a madness in his gaze. Octavia hisses and then moans at the pain, falling back onto the bed, and I increase my actions, drowning out the agony with blissful pleasure.

I grip her thigh tighter, and she begins to wriggle, her arousal dripping down my hand as I twist my fingers inside her, adding a fourth. It's a tight fit, but she lets me in, keening, her hips bucking.

"That's it, angel. I'm almost finished, and then you can come."

"I can't hold it," she says, panting heavier.

"Ten more seconds, and then come for us, sweetheart," Dorian orders.

I swirl my tongue over her clit, fucking melting as she cries my name, trying to buck harder into my face, my hand soaked. "Bastian!"

"Four seconds!" Dorian's voice is husky, and he grunts, a breathlessness in his tone that makes me think he's going to come as soon as she does.

"Dorian, please," she sobs, crying out as I do another flick of my tongue.

"Now, Octavia. Come now."

There's a slight pause, and then she shatters on my tongue, her legs shaking uncontrollably. I fuck her with my hand, hard and fast, curling my fingers until she squeezes them so tight, I think they might break. I pull them out, lifting my head with a gasp, rubbing her clit fast, watching as she squirts, covering me in her mess.

Dorian dives, dragging his tongue over his name marked on her thigh, capturing all the blood. He shivers, groaning, and I grasp him by the back of his neck, pulling his head to me, forcing the fingers that were just inside her into his mouth. He sucks them all the way to the back of his throat, running his tongue over every bit of skin. I grab his dick, squeezing it tight over his trousers, and smirk.

"Come for us, big brother."

His eyes flash, but a second later, his lashes flutter, and he shudders in my grip, falling on the bed, his trousers damping as he comes. I let him go, chuckling, stripping out of my clothes and crawl up Octavia's body.

"My turn, pretty girl."

She smiles, wrapping her arms around my neck, and I easily slip into her warm pussy, bottoming out in one swift movement.

"Fuck," I groan. "I want to live inside this pussy for the rest of my fucking life."

I grip her ass, being careful to hold her on the side without any marks, but she hisses anyway as I apply pressure to one of her tattoos. Her cunt clamps around my dick as I rock my hips, slowly grinding against her.

I keep my movements slow, gazing at her as she lies on the bed, her blonde hair fanned around her head like a halo. Her eyes are hooded, dazed with lust, pupils blown, lips swollen. She takes my fucking breath away. Something this beautiful loves me. She sees all my darkness, all my demons, and still loves me for it. Knows all my wrongs and doesn't care.

"I would die for you, Octavia. I would tear myself to shreds, condemning myself to the pits of hell, just to feel a minute of your love, to have you gaze at me the way you are just once."

I kiss her softly, pouring everything I have into it, letting her see into my tarnished soul.

"I love you, pretty girl," I whisper against her lips.

She runs her hands up my neck, digging them into my hair. "I love you, Bastian. I love all your faults, all your darkness. I don't love you despite those things, I love you for everything you are. Everything I have to give is yours."

I grab her face, pulling her against my lips as words get stuck in my throat. The moment is small and brief, as it shatters by my ass being invaded by something it didn't fucking invite in.

"Holy fucking christ," I grunt, snapping my head around.

Dorian kneels on the bed at our side, his clothes removed, stroking his cock as he holds what appears to be a knife, the handle penetrating my fucking ass with no warning or warm up. It fucking burns, but as I buck into Octavia, the burning only adds to my pleasure.

"Not nice when your moment is interrupted, is it?"

"Bastard," I snap, but it turns into a groan when he moves the knife, the handle hitting something inside that makes my legs weak. "Oh, fuck."

I dive down to capture Octavia's lips again, riding out the pleasure they're both giving me. Dorian fucks my ass, and Octavia grinds her hips, moving her pussy up and down on my dick, topping from the bottom. I've gone from being in charge to being the puppet at their mercy between them.

"Do you like that, big brother? Do you like him fucking your ass?" Octavia whispers against my lips, and I nod, unable to form any words. "Such a good boy. My good boy."

Her praise has shivers running down my spine at the same time her hands do, caressing me, soothing me, and I come undone. I roar against her shoulder, clamping my teeth down on her flesh, my hips stuttering as I come.

Didn't know I was such a praise whore.

Dorian rips the knife from my ass, and I cry out. My cheeks are spread, and then I feel warmth hitting me in between them. I limply twist to see him coming on my ass. He groans, working over every drop, all of it landing on me. He keeps me spread, staring me dead in the eye—or Octavia, I'm not sure, as she's raised her head to watch as well. He sticks his tongue out slowly, dragging it between my cheeks, licking his cum off.

My legs spasm when he circles it round my hole, I hiss out a breath and moan as Octavia's pussy clamps around my softening dick. Dorian takes the knife he had inside me and digs it into my flesh on the back of my thigh, marking me as he cleans me up with his tongue.

"Oh fuck," she whispers, trying to grind on me for some friction. I slip my hands between us, flicking and pinching her clit until she comes again, soaking me one more time.

I drop my head to her chest, resting there until Dorian is finished, and then place a soft kiss on her chest as he pats my ass. I roll off her, laying on my back in a fucking wonderful world of euphoria. Dorian starts to move up the bed, but Octavia sits up before I can even blink. She slaps him hard around the face; the sound ricocheting around the room. His head flies to the side, and he blinks rapidly, left dumbfounded for a moment, his left cheek sporting her handprint already.

I bolt up and move back slightly, giving her enough space to get a good swing so she doesn't mess it up. She huffs a laugh as I do so, shaking her head ever so slightly, and then her hand connects with my cheek. My head rings and my jaw clicks. Fuck, she put some power behind that. I grip my chin, working my jaw for a second, shaking my head to get rid of the ringing.

She sits on her knees between us, pointing a finger into our chests. "Don't you ever keep anything from me again that relates to me."

Dorian opens his mouth, but the heated look she gives him has him closing it.

"I don't want to hear your reasons for not telling me. I already bloody know them."

She does?

Her laughter is cold, reminding me so much of Dorian's, it's eerie. "At first, you wouldn't have told me because it was leverage on Father. Then, as you grew to care for me, I was yours, your little sister. No one was going to take the big brother role from you, and you would not want me to search for anybody else, or for me to care for anybody else."

Dorian cocks his head to the side, smirking at her, tipping his chin up. "And after our feelings changed?"

She tilts her head right back, raising an eyebrow. "That one is easy. You both liked the fucked up, twisted darkness of me wanting my full-blooded brothers and caving in." She laughs that cold laugh again and I swear, my dick is already hardening.

"I even get why you told Grandfather the way you did. It's one of your compulsions to do a damn villain monologue when you crush your target," she says, and Dorian scoffs, affronted. "Don't act like you don't. You've been doing it since we were kids. Bastian being the main recipient most of the time. You like to make everyone a puppet to your strings."

Dorian's mouth opens a couple times until he scowls, crossing his arms. "Well, how else are they supposed to know my genius? They don't work it out beforehand, so I have to tell them, it would take them years, if ever."

Rude.

Octavia's eyes soften, and she cups his cheek, rubbing her thumb over it. "I know, Rian. I know." She pushes her thumb in until he grunts, pinching his chin. "But never again to me," she says with malice in her tone.

Fuck. Yep, totally hard again.

I wrap my arms around her waist, pulling her onto my chest, laying back against the headboard. "Never again, pretty girl. I promise."

I raise my eyebrow at Dorian until he huffs, nodding in agreement. "You're right. I'm sorry, angel. I won't keep anything from you again."

"Good," she sighs, closing her eyes and relaxing in my hold. "Now that that's settled, can you please treat my wound? It is throbbing so freaking much."

Dorian gazes down at it, running his finger over the cut, tracing his name out before getting up and grabbing our medical kit from the closet.

"I'm going to need special treatment for my wound as well, *Rian*."

I squeeze Octavia tight, kissing her hair, taking a deep breath. "Just think: now, we can knock you up without you worrying something would be wrong with the baby. We're still related by blood, but it is so distant, it won't make a difference."

"No," Dorian bellows at the same time as she does.

"I don't want kids," she says, leaving no room for argument, looking up at me and Dorian. "I won't bring kids into this bloodline. Ever."

Dorian comes over with the kit, sitting down and placing the items he needs out. "Good, because I will never share you with another person apart from our brother. I can't."

The pained expression on his face shows that what he says is true. He will never be able to let her give a part of herself to another, never be able to handle her loving anyone but us. It's toxic and poisonous, but we've never tried to pretend we are anything but, and she loves us anyway.

"Bas?" she whispers, and I realise they are both waiting for me to say something, to acknowledge if I can live without children.

I shrug my shoulders, not caring either way. "I'm happy with whatever you want, pretty girl. Kid or no kid, it doesn't matter to me as long as you're getting what you want."

"This is what I want. Just us." She nods, closing her eyes, exhaustion taking over. Dorian cleans up her wound gently, and I close my eyes, content with my everything in my arms.

25

OCTAVIA

I lay in between Dorian and Bastian with my eyes closed, faking being asleep, waiting until they finally drift off. They would never let me do what I want to do alone, and I don't want them with me for this. This, I need to do by myself.

Bastian falls asleep first, snoring loudly, and Dorian follows closely behind, pulling me to him so tightly, I wouldn't be surprised if I was absorbed into his skin. I lay still for another few minutes, waiting until they're fully under, and then shuffle down the bed out of their grasp.

I stand at the edge of the bed, watching them for a moment, laughing silently as they frown, scooting forward in their sleep until they embrace and snuggle each other. They're so clingy in their sleep.

My hand brushes over the bandage on my leg, and I run my fingers across it, smiling. He carved Rian into my skin instead of Dorian. I guess he doesn't hate the nickname as much as I thought, or maybe he started to like it because I called him it. Either way, it feels even more special. He carved the shape of his dick onto Bastian's thigh and then sulked because Bas loved it. Twisted bastards.

I grab Dorian's discarded black shirt, slipping it on for something to wear, and slip out of the room, tiptoeing so as not to wake them. The halls are empty, everything quiet. There are no staff lurking in the shadows, no beady eyes watching to report back to someone. The castle is finally silent.

I trace my fingers along the walls as I go, in no rush to get to my destination. Grandfather will leave tomorrow but will be back in a week's time to discuss the wedding. I wonder if my wedding will come before the one he arranged that some other poor soul will end up being stuck in. I know of the Carter family; they're almost as brutal as us, bloody and vicious, and I'm glad I will not be ending up there.

Screams echo in the distance, bouncing off the walls as I descend the stairs, going deeper into the dungeon. My feet leave the plush carpet for the cold cement, and I shiver, regretting not putting on shoes. I follow the screams, gazing into the cells as I go, seeing so many people from my past. They have got every single person who ever hurt me down here, locked up to be tortured. If I know them, it will be a long time before they let anyone have the peace of death.

A loud bang and a final scream come from the room on my left a few doors down. A sickening wet squelch has my stomach turning, and I scrunch up my nose, peering inside to see someone with their head caved in laid on the floor. The person is unrecognisable, bones, blood, and teeth splattered against a wall.

"I hope they deserved it," I say, leaning against the door frame.

Ghost snaps his head up, wiping blood from his face, smearing it all over. "I wondered if they would let you come see me."

I laugh, shaking my head, crossing my arms across my chest. "They would never let me come see you alone. I waited until they were asleep. They wouldn't suspect I would seek you out after just learning that *you* were actually the one who contributed your sperm to my existence. It was the only time to get you alone."

"And you wanted to speak with me alone?" he asks, grabbing a wooden chair, pushing out another from the small table at the back of the room, gesturing for me to take a seat.

I walk into the room, feeling the blood and other things I don't want to think about between my toes, seriously regretting not putting on shoes. I grab the chair he offered, and we sit down at the same time.

"I wanted to speak with you without having to deal with those two. You'd be dead before I even got my first few questions out."

He nods his head, huffing a laugh. "That sounds like them."

"How did they find out you were my biological father? Did you tell them?" I ask, not bothering to beat around the bush.

He grasps my chin with his bloody hands, and I lift it, clenching my jaw. "Dorian noticed first. Saw me watching you too closely. 'You have her eyes,' he said. I had never been more terrified of a child than when I thought he was going to blow my identity."

He lets me go, and I rub my chin, unable to stop myself from looking at his eyes, seeing my own reflected. How have I never seen that before?

"But he didn't. He walked away and never mentioned it again. It wasn't until you got older, and we started to work more closely to protect you, that I told him I had been sent by Vincent to be his spy. Vincent Stone never trusted his son and wanted a more trained soldier in the manor to take care of things if the need should arise."

"You call what you did protecting me?" I ask, tilting my head to the side. "I was terrified of you when I was younger."

He runs his hand through his hair, smearing the white-blonde with blood. "What I did was to protect you, to make you stronger. I saw so much of my sister in you. She was soft, kind, and belonged far away, but she couldn't get away and she died because she couldn't survive this life."

His voice shakes, and he coughs, clearing his throat. "She took her own life because she didn't see another way out, and I was too late to save her. I didn't want to take the chance of making the same mistake with you."

His hand reaches across the table and hesitantly grabs mine. I don't hold it back, but I don't shake him off either.

"Your mother, Lucinda, and I were just a brief fling, something to do to pass the time, and then one day she told me she was getting married to Charles Stone. I thought nothing of it, of her until your birth and her death were announced. I thought the timing odd but didn't look too deeply into it. I didn't want to if I'm honest, but then I saw you at one of your birthday balls, you were three years old and all I saw was my sister. I knew you were mine, knew I had to protect you."

"You never tried to take me. You never tried to get me away from this place," I say and he hears the accusation in my tone and drops my hand like I burned him.

"Would you have gone if I tried? Would you have left them behind?" He points to the ceiling, indicating to the only two people I care about. "By the time I arrived, they were your everything. You only smiled when they were around, seeking them out even when it got you punished. You would have never left them."

I nod, conceding that he is correct. I wouldn't have left them, I would have put up so much of a fight to stay with them he would have been caught. Still...

"Shouldn't that have been irrelevant? Shouldn't you have cared enough to want more for me than a life in the bloodline, done everything you could have physically done?"

He works his jaw, avoiding my gaze, and I know I'm right.

"You did what you could while still keeping yourself safe. You toed the line of risking being banished or slaughtered by the bloodline, but you didn't fully go over it." He opens his mouth to either object or make an excuse, but I wave my hand, cutting him off.

"Look I get it, there's only two people I would stick my life on the line for in this fucked up organisation. But they are also the only ones that would for me as well. I just needed to confirm that," I say, standing up.

I'm not sure what I was hoping to get talking to him or what I even wanted, but I feel like I got it.

"I do care about you, Octavia," he shouts, jumping to his feet, his hands planted on the table. "I...I wish I could say more. I wish..." His face scrunches up, his nostrils flaring.

"I know," I whisper. "Maybe you'll care about someone else one day enough to save them, but it's okay that it wasn't me. I never needed saving."

I grasp the door frame, biting the bottom lip, needing to do one more thing, cause I might not need saving but he does.

"You should leave the manor," I say, twisting to look back at him. "If they think that for a second I might come to care about you, they're going to kill you. I wouldn't risk staying too long."

He nods his head over to a corner of the room near where the dead body lays and there are two duffle bags. "Already figured my time here was done. I never expected to last as long as I did. I just wanted to see you before I went."

Ah, he was already planning on going and not sticking around. Figures.

"Take care of yourself, little mouse."

"Goodbye, Ghost."

I walk away, not looking back, settled in the last conversation I will have with him. I doubt I'll ever see him again. He'll have to lie low for a while, seeing as he betrayed the head of the bloodline, and I doubt he cares enough to risk coming back.

Coming up from the stairs, I spot Dorian and Bastian leaning against a wall in only their boxers, arms crossed, waiting for me.

"Little sister, breaking the rules again?" Dorian tuts.

"Isn't that what little sisters do?" I smile, rushing towards them. They catch me in their grasp, holding me so tight, I know they will never let me go.

"I think we need to kill the bastard right fucking now," Bastian growls, and I laugh, shaking my head.

Knew it.

"No," I tell them. "He's leaving. I had to have one last conversation with him before he left, but he's going now, and he won't be coming back."

"And you're okay with that?" Dorian asks, studying me. They cup a cheek each, making me look at them, checking to see if I'll lie.

"I've never needed anyone but the two of you. My demons of Velka Manor."

"Only yours," Bastian whispers, pulling me between them.

"And you are only ours," Dorian growls as they consume me in their embrace, giving me no room to breathe, move, or see any of the world outside of them.

I wouldn't want it any other way.

26

OCTAVIA

I was born for my brothers.

That is why I exist: to belong to them.

Our damage is something you can never fix, the wounds scarring our souls until they're ruined beyond repair. We've been twisted up from the inside, but in the darkness, we found each other, forging our broken parts together until we are only whole together.

I was born for them, but they live for me. Every decision, every action, I am at the centre. They don't do anything unless it benefits our life together. Without me, they would be lost. They would have no peace, no love, just darkness until the sweet release of death took them. Without them, I would be nothing—a shell without a soul, drifting through life until it ended.

I wasn't supposed to love them, and they weren't supposed to love me, but the world pushed us together in a way I will never regret.

"What is our blushing bride doing out here all alone?" Dorian whispers in my ear, his haunting voice sending goosebumps down my spine as I admire the beautiful art Bastian painted on my nails the night before—pink and black roses with blood dripping down thorns. I'm obsessed with them.

"Not thinking about running, are you, pretty girl?" Bastian growls, coming up behind me on my other side. "Because we would be more than happy to hunt you down." He grazes his teeth over my bare shoulder, biting down until I moan, tilting my head back into his chest.

"You're supposed to be waiting for me at the *end* of the aisle," I whisper, melting into their touch.

"Did you really think we would let you walk down the aisle without having a taste?" Dorian groans, placing me between them with him at my front. "You're all dressed up like the most beautiful treat I've ever seen."

He eyes up my blush pink wedding dress, running his fingers over the exposed skin of my chest. Bastian cups my breasts in the corset, gripping them tight, running his lips over the shell of my ear. "I want to stand at the end of the aisle with you all over my fucking face."

"Do you want your big brothers to eat your pussy and your ass before you tie yourself to us for the rest of our lives?" Dorian asks, tipping my chin up with his finger.

"Yes," I moan, panting as Bastian pulls up the big skirt of my dress, bending down and cursing as he gets a glimpse underneath.

"Naughty fucking girl, getting married with no underwear on. I want your cum dripping down your legs as you say I do. Tell me what you want, angel."

I lick my lips, my pupils blown wide, holding in the moan as Bastian drags his tongue over my cheeks. "You. I want both of my big brothers to make me come."

"Good fucking girl," Dorian growls, capturing my mouth, sucking on my bottom lip before dropping to his knees.

I lean forward, placing my hands on the wooden door that separates us from a room full of people waiting to watch us get married. Dorian kisses the scar of his name on my thigh, then the other one where I let Bastian carve his as well. Can't have one without the other.

Bastian spreads my ass, his tongue teasing my hole, making my legs shake and a gasp fly free. He's so fucking good at that. Bastian's tongue was made to worship my body. Dorian flattens his tongue on my clit, swirling it in a circle, doing that thing I love with his fingers. He slips two inside me and then stretches them out as far as they will go, making me feel so full before adding a third.

My wavy hair starts to stick to my skin, sweat beading as heat builds. They both lick and suck and bite, making every nerve inside me come alive. I bite my bottom lip, trying to hold in the noises I'm making. Every single important person in the bloodline is just on the other side of the doors I'm leaning against. Our wedding has become the event of the century—not one person RSVP'd no. We even had people send in requests to come who weren't invited. Everyone wants to know how this has been allowed to happen, but no one has had the courage to voice their concerns, according to my grooms.

"Oh fuck," I moan, slamming my hand over my mouth. Dorian has worked my pussy so much, I feel his fifth finger slip in, and I feel so full, I fear I'm going to burst as Bastian slips two fingers into my ass.

"Don't you dare cover your mouth, pretty girl," Bastian growls, sinking his teeth into my ass cheek. "We want them all to hear how much we make you scream."

They both pick up the speed, not leaving me empty for a second. My legs shake, lightning shoots down my spine, roaring pleasure filling me up from my toes. Dorian moves his head back, flicking my clit with his other hand as he fists me.

"Come for us, angel. Show them all who you belong to."

My orgasm rolls through me, stronger than it's ever been. My back bows, my head flying back as I scream. They keep going, not letting the orgasm die out. Dorian fucks me with his fist vigorously until my legs begin to shake and my knees buckle. He pulls out his hand, and I come all over his face.

"Oh god," I sob, about to fall to the ground, but they both jump up, catching me in their embrace.

"Not God, angel. Your fucking brothers are the only ones who make you come like that," Dorian whispers harshly, licking up the side of my neck.

Bastian leans over my shoulder and drags his tongue over Dorian's chin, catching my release before kissing me on the lips so I can taste all three of us.

"Let's go get fucking hitched." He grins against my lips. My dress falls back into place, but before I even have a chance to fix myself up properly, Bastian opens the double doors, slamming them hard against the wall so every single person in the room turns back to us in shock. From the looks on their faces, there wasn't a single soul that didn't just hear me scream.

"You are supposed to meet me at the end of the aisle," I hiss quietly as they stand on either side of me, each taking an arm.

"Like we'd ever let anyone else have the honour of escorting you down." Dorian places a quick kiss on my lips and winks. "I'd kill them if they tried."

Bastian cackles loudly. "You're ours, pretty girl. No one touches you."

He smacks a loud kiss on my lips, and then the music starts to play, and my grooms walk me toward the start of our future.

***

The wedding went off without a hitch. No one objected, no one said a word or even blinked when the officiant said *I now pronounce you husbands and wife, you may now kiss your sister.* They specifically requested he phrase it like that. I'm not sure how legal this wedding is—the person who married us belongs to the bloodline and conducts every ceremony, but I don't know how real it can be marrying three people, let alone when they all have the same father on their birth certificates. It doesn't matter to me, though. I've never not been theirs.

"Beautiful ceremony," a timber voice says, coming up to my side. My grooms narrow their eyes from across the room where they went to get me food, eyeing our grandfather, but I smile to reassure them.

"It was," I say, turning towards him. "Thank you for all your help arranging it."

"You're very welcome, granddaughter." He bows his head, bending to kiss my cheek, placing something small in my hand. "I hope my present is to your liking."

A waiter brings over four glasses of champagne, and he selects two, passing one to me while the waiter leaves the other two for my grooms.

"Oh, I'm sure it is." I grin, clutching my hand, slipping the two gifts into the drinks. "If there is anything wrong with the presents, I will finish what my brother started," I warn, eyeing him carefully.

He bellows a laugh that makes me start. I don't think I've ever heard him laugh. "Don't worry, Octavia. It's exactly what you asked for. I'm actually looking forward to seeing what both your brothers, or should I say husbands, will do in the future."

We watch them coming towards us, Bastian scowling, Dorian with a cold, hard mask of emotions. He kisses me on the cheek one more time with a wink. "It gets boring at the top without competition. I think the next few years will be rather fun."

He walks away just as my husbands get closer, turning once more to look at me up and down before sighing. "Pink? Really?" he tuts, shaking his head, and I laugh.

He actually played a major part in arranging this wedding and came dress shopping with me a few times. He wanted black but said he would settle for white. So of course I went with pink. I saw a side to him that was slightly tolerable, if you can forget what an evil, cold-blooded human he is.

"Everything okay, pretty girl?" Bastian wraps his arm around my waist, glaring at our grandfather's retreating back.

I smile up at him, handing him a drink. "Everything is perfect."

Dorian guides us over to our table, placing the food down, and I give him his drink. He eyes it for a few seconds, and I do my best to keep my face even. He finally takes a sip, and I hold in my breath of relief.

"What are you planning, little wife?" he asks, raising an eyebrow.

I grab his tie, stand on my tiptoes, and bite his bottom lip, dragging it into my mouth. "I'm just wondering how long we have to stay here before I can drag my husbands away so they can fuck me until I can't move."

"Naughty, pretty girl." Bastian laughs, kissing up my neck.

"One more hour," Dorian grunts, grabbing my chin and licking the seams of my lips. "One more hour, and I'm going to fuck you in this room, whether we have an audience or not."

I giggle, pulling them both closer, letting their lips worship me as I begin the countdown, but it most definitely won't be an hour.

Thirty minutes go by, and it finally starts to take effect. Dorian and Bastian are slumped in their chairs, a glazed look in their eyes. I nod my head towards my grandfather, and he and his men make quick work emptying the ballroom. While they do that, I quickly sneak away to get changed.

The clothes were all laid out for me in the bathroom, so it doesn't take me long. As I walk back into the ballroom, I hear them both screaming my name. The wings on my back drag across the floor, black feathers floating around me. I had them specially made, and they were so worth the cost. My thigh high black boots clack against the floor, my hips swaying with every step. I place my hands over my hips in the black corset, with only booty shorts to cover my ass.

"Octavia!" Dorian roars, his head flying from side to side.

"Where is she? Where is she?" Bastian stamps his foot before yelling, jumping to the side. "Damn, fucking snakes are everywhere. We need to find her. The snakes want her, but she's ours."

He stamps his foot on the ground, killing the imaginary snakes. "You can't fuck her, you slithering bastards. She's ours, not yours."

"The clocks are ticking. We need to find her, the clocks are ticking," Dorian groans, pulling at his hair.

I slip my mask on, putting my fingers between my lips and whistle. They twist around, a feral snarl on their lips, pupils dilated.

Dorian falls to his knees, his head lifting as I get closer. "Dark angel," he whispers.

I ignore him, grabbing Bastian by his chin, moving him next to Dorian. "Kneel," I bark when he does nothing. He drops to his knees with a bang, groaning as I run my hands through his hair. "Good boy."

I walk around them slowly, enjoying their rapid breathing, their shivers as I drag my nails across their backs. I grip both of their chins, pulling their heads up to face me as I lean down.

"You didn't think I would forget about all my nightmares, did you, husbands?"

I fling them backwards, and they fall onto their backs, slowly pushing themselves away from me. I pull a large, gleaming knife from behind my back, the light catching it.

"Welcome to *my* fright night at Velka Manor, big brothers. I'm going to make you scream."

They both groan, grabbing their cocks, panting as I drag my tongue over the knife, not letting my eyes off them for a second.

"Run," I whisper.

They bolt up and run as fast as they can, and I giggle as they push each other, tripping over everything and nothing. I skip along after them, ready to show them they're not the only demons who live in the castle of sin anymore.

I fucking love my life.

"One, two, your dark angel is coming for you..."

AFTERWORD

T hank you much for reading Velka Manor, I hoped you enjoyed Octavia, Dorian, and Bastian's twisted love story. I want to thank my amazing friend and book cover designer Jes for creating me such an amazing cover, I have been in love and obsessed with it since the moment she created it, and my fantastic editor Alexa for getting this story to were it is now. I also want to thank my fantastic beta readers Shakala, Dayamara, and Frankie, this book wouldn't have come out without you. And a big thank you to my ARC readers for staying with me on the delay and taking a chance on this book. Love you guys.

If you want to follow me for at all for more stories in the bloodline and more forbidden & tab00 stories, follow me at the places below.
https://www.instagram.com/winterbrierauthor/
https://www.facebook.com/winterbrierauthor

Printed in Dunstable, United Kingdom